He Had Ruined Everything!

"We've got to get back to our party, which may be much trickier than getting in here was." Jessie chuckled.

"It's okay for you to laugh, but what would my clients think of me coming out of a darkened room in this shape . . . holding my wife's hand?" he teased back. Then he felt her stiffen in his arms. "Jessie?"

"It would be much more acceptable if you were with someone else, wouldn't it, Philip? More macho and far more titillating." She unlocked the door swiftly, then opened it. "Thanks for the interlude."

Then she was gone.

RITA CLAY

has tried almost every job once. This former bookstore manager also sold cosmetics, worked in a bank and ran her own modeling school before turning to writing. Now a successful romance author, she looks forward to describing the diversity and joys of love in many books to come.

Dear Reader:

SILHOUETTE DESIRE is an exciting new line of contemporary romances from Silhouette Books. During the past year, many Silhouette readers have written in telling us what other types of stories they'd like to read from Silhouette, and we've kept these comments and suggestions in mind in developing SILHOUETTE DESIRE.

DESIREs feature all of the elements you like to see in a romance, plus a more sensual, provocative story. So if you want to experience all the excitement, passion and joy of falling in love, then SILHOUETTE DESIRE is for you.

Meredith Morgan,
Silhouette Books,
320 Steelcase Rd., East,
Markham, Ontario
L3R 2M1

RITA CLAY
Recapture The Love

Silhouette Desire

Published by Silhouette Books New York

Distributed in Canada by PaperJacks Ltd., a Licensee
of the trademarks of Simon & Schuster, Inc.

This is for three very important men in my life:
Jeff and Greg Abrams, my brothers, for always
giving me such wonderful support no matter
what I wanted to try. And to my dad, Dan Clay,
who gave me my first typewriter.
Thanks, guys!

SILHOUETTE BOOKS, a Division of Simon & Schuster, Inc.
1230 Avenue of the Americas, New York, N.Y. 10020
In Canada distributed by PaperJacks Ltd.,
330 Steelcase Road, Markham, Ontario

Copyright © 1984 by Rita Clay

Distributed by Pocket Books

ISBN: 0-671-44375-5

First Silhouette Books printing February, 1984

10 9 8 7 6 5 4 3 2 1

1

Someone was watching her.

Jessie Young stood under the dim street lamp in the early dark of downtown Dallas. She glanced over her shoulder, hoping to put her fears to rest. Her bus was ten minutes late, and she was the only commuter who had decided to wait it out. Perhaps she was a fool to hope the misty rain would clear up and she would get home from work on time—just once.

She glanced around again, forcing herself to dismiss her feelings as nonsense. There were a few men with dark umbrellas hurrying down the almost-deserted sidewalks as they searched out parking lots or taxis. One or two men in trench coats stood in doorways to get out of the damp wind as they discussed last-minute details of the day's business transactions. They were obviously in no hurry, either, to reach the warm hearth of home or battle the cold December rain.

Then her darting eyes rested in instant recognition on the sleek gray Cadillac parked across the street.

Philip.

She heard the engine roar, then watched the car as it pulled into the mainstream of traffic and wove its way toward her. With a feeling of inevitability, she waited. There was no use ignoring him, because she knew, deep down inside, that she would have to see him sometime. Now was just as good a time as any. Thoughts flitted through her mind, only to move down to the pit of her stomach and form a hard ball of nerves. They had been married twelve years, yet during the past three months, since she had left him, there had been more changes in their lives than in all those years. Was he the same? Would he notice the change in her? Would he care? Did *she* care? She didn't know.

The door was snapped open, and a deep voice moved her to action. "Get in before you drown."

She slipped onto the rich velvet upholstered seat next to him, ignoring the fact that her wet raincoat was blotting the plush material and turning it to a darkened black gray. He could afford to have it redone if necessary.

His pale brown eyes quickly scanned her body from head to foot before he turned his attention to the traffic. They drove in quiet, formal silence. Although she prayed for it to last, she knew that it wouldn't exist for long. Philip never allowed an opportunity to pass without telling her to come home, where he thought she belonged.

"You've lost a lot of weight," he finally commented, his rough voice resounding in the emptiness of the car.

"Twenty-five pounds.".

"Too much."

"I still have five more to go."

"Are you starving yourself from ego or economics?"

"Both." She knew that would hit him.

"You cut your hair, too."

"It's easier to keep this way." And it went better with the new image of a career woman she was trying so hard to create, she added silently.

"Do you need money?"

"Yes, and as soon as I'm promoted to manager and earn it, I'll have it. Most of us work on commission, you know, just as you do."

"Attorneys don't work on commission, Jessie. Our fees are set by the type of work we do, not how much we do."

"It's the same principle, Philip," she said tiredly. All she wanted was a hot bath and a bowl of equally hot soup. She could taste it. Perhaps she'd have chicken noodle or tomato. . . .

"You're not listening!"

"And you're shouting. After twelve years of marriage, does that make us even?"

He was silent again, his expression closed and distant as he negotiated his way off the main road and onto the freeway that led to her apartment complex.

"I'm sorry, Jessie. Every time I say I'm going to be patient with you, I lose my patience. What I really wanted to say is that I'd like you to come home and spend the weekend with the girls and me. I'm having a small get-together for my parents' anniversary. I know they'd love to have you join us." He hesitated just a breath's time, then continued in an even faster voice. "We could give the semblance of being a family for the sake of the children. I think they need to see us together occasionally. This way you'd still have the children for the weekend, and we'd have your company."

"I'm not moving back, Philip. I've told you that over and over until I'm tired of hearing myself say it." Adrenaline flowed like a jet stream through her body as she felt the sheer but strongly woven net of their now-tattered marriage hanging over her head.

"Is there another man? Is that it?" His voice tightened with anger.

Jessie didn't answer. What could she say? No, there wasn't anyone. Her boss occasionally treated her to a meal, but the conversation always concerned business. No, better to say nothing at all than let him know just how unsocial she had become.

His hands tightened on the wheel as he turned the corner that led to her apartment. "Don't worry, I'm not asking you to move in forever. I'm only requesting the honor of your presence for the weekend." His voice was edged in bitterness. "Obviously, it isn't a commitment for a lifetime. You wouldn't honor it if it were."

"Don't, Philip." She strengthened her grip on

the door handle as he angled the car toward the curb. "I appreciate the ride home, but I won't pay my taxi fare by allowing you to slice me apart with words that have been said over and over. I'll call and let you know my decision tomorrow." She turned to slide out; then, for some reason she couldn't express, stopped, looked over her shoulder and stared directly into his eyes. He looked tired, too. His wavy, lion's-mane-colored hair was slightly mussed; his chin showed the beginning of a shadowed stubble. His gray three-piece suit was wilted and discolored by the rain. She wanted to comfort him, to hold him in her arms and rock him until his hurt went away.

And she wanted to kill him for his past infidelities, real or imagined. Her heart stopped beating for a moment as the ache returned. A deep, almost overwhelming pain seared through to her soul for all that they had lost. Then she almost visibly pushed the crowding images behind her and stiffened her resolve. "Good-by, Philip. I'll let you know about the weekend. Thanks for the ride."

She slowly climbed the outside stairs to her second-story apartment, her feet dragging in the drizzle. It had been three months since she had last seen him. Three months of feeling the intense loss of his presence. She was finally at the point of going to bed without curling up holding a pillow that she dreamed took on the shape of him. She was learning to be independent, on her own, self-sufficient.

She opened the door and flipped on the light, dropping her purse and coat on the closest chair.

She slipped her shoes off and padded across the small living room to the minuscule kitchen where she put some water on to boil. Whether she made tea or soup, she'd need to have hot water. Then she curled up on the couch, only to stare out the window at the dark clouds beyond.

Philip. Two years earlier, her world had revolved around him. No, that wasn't true, her conscience corrected. Her world had revolved around his world. And she had been as much at fault for that as he had. She had played the part of mother of three and wife to Philip Young, successful attorney, to the hilt. Her clothing was bought at the right boutiques, she played bridge with the right people, and she stumbled around the tennis courts with other wives of up-and-coming executives who were there for the same reasons. Then their son had died in a crazy, needless auto accident on his way home from a baseball game, and the sun had stopped shining. P.J. had been a miniature of Philip, with his light, sun-kissed hair, a winsome smile that had wrapped around her heart and a way of making the day come alive. For Jessie, it had become a constant rainy season. No one else could calculate her loss, and when others offered support and sympathy, she pushed them away with total disregard for their feelings. After all, what could they know about a pain that raged through her entire being like a thousand sharp knives? They had never been in her position.

She attempted to piece her world together again, but only in spurts. Philip had tried to console her, but he had only made things worse. He had been lucky; he still had his work in which to bury himself. But she had nothing, she kept telling herself. She had suffered the one loss a mother dreads most: her favored child.

Then she had found a hotel key and a note in one of Philip's suit pockets. The key was from the Fairmont, a prestigious hotel in the heart of Dallas. The note was from a client's ex-mistress: Catherine Sinclair, a country and Western singer who had made it big, a woman with a great voice and an even greater appetite for men. And she had apparently decided that she wanted Philip Young. Later, Jessie had found out that Catherine wasn't the only one who had had designs on her husband, but by that time, she had already left him, and the information had only reconfirmed for her the rightness of her earlier decision. Her other reasons for leaving were as varied and confused as her thoughts. All she knew was that she had to run or lose her own sanity. Peace was what she needed. That, and time to think.

The water bubbled, hitting the burner with a hissing sound, and Jessie was jolted out of her reverie. She opened a packet of dry soup and mixed it into the boiling water, then turned to sit down again and remember. Remember.

When she had confronted Philip, he hadn't denied the fact that Catherine had propositioned him. He *had* denied taking her up on her offer. What had hurt most was that he was so open about the temptation. What had he said? "Yes, damn it! I did come close to making love to her in that room! Every time I turned to you for comfort, you pulled away! You enjoy being miserable and shutting me out! Well, I need some compassion, too! I need you, Jessie; only you're not there!''

They had tried to patch together what had been torn apart in grief, but after a month, Jessie had known that the seams of their marriage wouldn't hold together under the strain. She had loved him with all her heart, but it just wasn't enough to keep that insecure, unstable part of herself from doubting, wondering, questioning, demanding. She kept wondering how many other offers he had been handed and how many of those he had taken up. After all, he was a handsome, successful man by anyone's standards. And he had traveled extensively under the guise of business. But she couldn't force herself to confront the problem by putting it into words. Nor could she face examining the other less spectacular but just as important issues that had slowly but inevitably eaten away at their relationship. Within the space of a morning, she had packed and moved out, leaving Philip with both their girls and the house and cars. She had decided that the children had coped with enough upheaval in their young lives and that changing schools and home would only add to their feelings of instability and confusion. Besides, she needed breathing room to find out who she was and what she wanted from life. She even needed to know if she wanted to live.

For the past three months, she had collected the

children from the housekeeper every Friday evening before Philip came home and dropped them off on Sunday evening, never entering the house or confronting her husband. And now he wanted her to spend the weekend there, with him.

Was it a ruse? Was it a trick to keep her there? She smiled ruefully to herself. How in the world would he do that? There were no prison doors. However, that tiny but intimate fear remained. Would she walk through the door, willing only to spend a weekend, and instantly become as complacent as she had once been, content to drift along with nowhere as her goal and nothing holding her interest? She unconsciously straightened her shoulders. Well, now was the time to find out. She had to finally face her family and see if she could cope with them and the life they led without her, or she would always wonder whether she had done the right thing by leaving.

In the morning, she would call Philip and tell him that she'd love to spend the weekend with them, as a family.

But for now she would sip her soup, take a hot shower, do her exercises and go to bed. Sleep would be another matter entirely.

The next morning, Jessie's less-than-steady hand dialed Philip's office. She clenched the receiver tightly to her ear as she waited for his secretary to put her through.

"Philip Young here."

"Hello, Philip?" Jessie's voice was cool and

calm. It was her stomach that was upset. "This is Jessie," she said unnecessarily. "What time would you like me to be there Friday?"

"I'll pick you up after work," he said, his voice as brisk and businesslike as hers was impersonal.

Damn him! She had lain awake all night planning this phone call! Couldn't he at least act excited that she had decided to come? "Your enthusiasm overwhelms me," she said dryly, before thinking how he would interpret her words.

"Every time I get too close, you back away, Jessie. I'm trying my damndest not to make you panic." His voice was weary, but she refused to allow him to touch that small part of her that wanted to react with kindness and loving. It also reacted to hurt and disappointment, and she couldn't handle that yet.

"Oh? Do I show signs of acting that flighty?" Her voice was caustic. It was the only weapon she had.

"No, your stability sticks out a mile," he replied, mimicking her tone.

"All right, Philip. I give up. I should have remembered never to argue with a lawyer."

He hesitated a minute, apparently thinking of saying something to that, then abruptly changed his mind and went on. "I'll see you Friday, Jessie. And thank you for agreeing. I think we both need to help the children get used to this arrangement."

"Has there been any trouble?" Her voice showed her instant concern.

"No, not really, but Beth is so quiet lately. She hardly talks or laughs anymore. And Amy is constantly into things. I think their boat has been rocked too much in the past month, with me traveling."

"Trips for Noah Weston to see Catherine Sinclair?" she replied cattily. Philip had represented Noah Weston, one of the wealthiest men in Dallas, and his various businesses for years. At one time, Noah had owned a record company, and Catherine was his star singer.

"You're half right, at least," he said. "But it's not a topic for this conversation. I'll see you Friday."

Philip decreed that the conversation was over, and it was over, Jessie thought as she slowly hung up the phone.

Was she doing the right thing by spending a weekend with him now, when she was just gaining a small measure of confidence in herself and her own abilities? She didn't know, but her heart cried out to see her children. She had so little time with them, anyway, that one missed weekend was too long. And if she refused to go to Philip's and took the children, it would hurt them, because then they would miss their grandparents' party. She had no choice. She had to go. She wondered if Philip knew that. He probably did, she realized wearily. After all, he was one of the top attorneys in Dallas, or Noah Weston wouldn't have him.

She turned around and placed her best plastic smile on her face. "Can I help you?" she asked the customer who was glancing through the rack of new designer dresses. She was determined to make her sales quota despite the fact that she wanted to hide in a hole and catch up on her lost sleep. She'd make a success of herself if it killed her!

"Have you packed a long gown?" Philip eyed the small leather suitcase standing in the center of the floor.

Jessie stood at the entrance to the kitchen. She had dressed in her best, a pale champagne-colored suit over a rust bow-tied blouse that enhanced the impact of her copper-colored hair. Her makeup was perfect; she had worked on it for a full hour. Her shoes were made of alligator, as was her handbag. She looked terrific, and she knew it. But all he could comment on was the contents of her suitcase!

"Aren't your parents' affairs always formal?" She answered his question with a question, something that she knew had always bothered him.

He gave her an exasperated look. "I didn't mean to imply that you wouldn't be dressed properly. It's just that the suitcase is so small."

"I'm only spending two days, Philip. I told you, I'm not moving back in." She struck back at him without thinking. "Didn't your girl friends travel light when they went away with you?" Why bother to explain that the gown was a clinging, un-wrinklable jersey that could be rolled into a small ball?

His face turned to stone, his eyes flinty in their hardness. "That was bitchy and uncalled for, Jessie," was all he said as he reached for the strap to her case.

She watched the light catch his blond hair,

18

turning it golden, and her fingers itched to reach out and touch it, to feel the strong, springy texture of it. She had to keep her feet from marching toward him so she could hold him, feel him close to her again.

"You're right, and I apologize. This weekend we will not discuss your indiscretions. They've been talked about enough over the past year," she promised with equal acerbity. "This weekend belongs to your parents and my children. And not necessarily in that order."

"That's what's always endeared you to me. Your caring attitude toward others."

Suddenly, she felt small. He had only asked one simple question, and she had gone into her same old act. When would she learn? "I'm sorry. I didn't mean to take my nervousness out on you."

He looked astonished. "Nervousness? What have you got to be nervous about? You look terrific; you're spending the weekend with your own kids; you know me, and you know my parents." She could tell that he was honestly puzzled by her comment.

She took a deep breath. If she was going to salvage this weekend and ultimately take her destiny into her own hands, she knew she would have to be honest with herself—and Philip. "Look, I know I look terrific, but I don't feel terrific—I feel fat and frumpy, the way I used to be. I know I'm seeing the kids, but I feel like a traitor for having left them with you in the first place, even though we agreed that they're much better off with you at our house than having their lives changed around by living with me. I like your parents, but I can't help wondering if they're sitting in judgment of my actions and will show me just how they feel about my leaving their 'golden boy who can do no wrong.'"

A slow, wicked grin that reached up to twinkle in his golden-brown eyes totally disarmed her. "That's the first honest reaction I've had from you in ages," he said in a low voice. "Perhaps we're getting somewhere, after all." His smile continued, making her distinctly uncomfortable as he opened the door and ushered her out with a flourish. "And I accept your very gracious apology."

It took her time while she got in the car and Philip started the engine to realize that his attitude had also changed. A year before, he would have ranted at her for childish behavior. This time he had called her a bitch. She'd grown up in his eyes. She gave a small, secret smile. Who would have thought that she would be called a bitch and take it as a compliment?

It was almost dinner time when they arrived at the house. The two-story English-style home was ablaze with lights shining from every window. Bright red Christmas lights framed the door and roof and gave the house the cheery, festive air it always had at the holiday season.

"You're still supporting the power company, I see," she mentioned dryly, and he chuckled.

"Amy is afraid of the dark and makes sure that we all have sufficient lighting. The housekeeper's grocery list holds a constant reminder for her to get light bulbs."

"You need to be more firm with her, Philip. Having every other light on would do just as well."

Suddenly, his chuckle was buried in his throat. "She's got enough on her plate right now. Light bulbs can always be replaced."

She stiffened, not willing to take all the blame. "Are you implying that Amy's problem is my fault?"

Philip pulled the car into the driveway and killed the engine before turning toward her. "No, I'm saying that she doesn't have your help to scare away the ominous presence of death," he said quietly in the darkness of the car. "We all lost P.J. to a senseless accident, Jessie. Not just you. And we all show it in different ways. Amy shows her fear by wanting the lights on. Beth is showing hers by her silence." He hesitated for just a moment. "And you showed yours by running away."

"I didn't run away. I ran to meet life, and perhaps, with luck, find myself," she answered candidly. She had never spoken to him that way before. "I found that I didn't know who I was or where I was going. How could I cope with the children's problems when I couldn't even cope with my own?" She searched for the words to make her explanation understood. "I couldn't even maintain a semblance of a household schedule. I never remembered when to pick up the children or the groceries or even your laundry." Mentioning his laundry brought back the memory of the note she had found in the suit jacket she had been readying for the cleaners. She froze as the sheer horror of that scene flooded back. And with it came the terrible, heart-wrenching hurt and anguish. Suddenly, the door that had begun to open between them was slammed shut. "But I'm learning."

Philip leaned toward her, his golden-brown eyes imploring. "Jessie, don't shut me out. Please. I want to understand, to help, but you won't let me get through to you." His voice was low, gravelly, as he attempted to knock down her wall of resistance, but he could see that it was too late. Whatever she had thought of had turned her back into herself, and there was no path for him to follow to find her again.

"I don't think there's any more to say. Can we go in now?" Her voice was stiff, matching her backbone.

"No, damn it! I want to talk! Talk to me, Jessie! Tell me what it is that you want from me, the girls, life, anything! But talk to me!"

"I want to be left alone! I want you to stop hounding me as if I were some criminal you want to prosecute! I want you to stay out of my life and let me make my own mistakes, not yours! Can't you leave me alone?" she ended with a quaver, trying hard to control herself and at the same time control him. But she couldn't. He wouldn't be controlled.

"And I want you, Jessie. We can work things out; I know we can. I'm just not sure anymore what the problems are. Do you want to work? Is that it? All right, I'll let you work!"

"That's just it, Philip. I don't need your permission! I'm not one of your children, nor your mother, who dotes on every pearl of wisdom that falls from your mouth. I don't need anything from you."

There was a tense silence as they each waited expectantly for the other to react. Jessie wished he would say something, anything, that would take the strain away from their aborted beginning. But she knew that nothing could be unsaid or undone.

Philip reached for the automatic lock and released the doors. Before she was out of the car, he was grabbing for her small suitcase, then slamming the door with all the frustration he must have felt.

They walked across the lawn and toward the front door, staying at least a foot apart, as if the ground between them were electrified. Just before they reached the door, Jessie could hear six-year-old Amy shouting, "It's Mommy! Mommy's here, Beth; Mommy's here!"

The door swung open, and Amy stood on the well-lit porch, her expression showing her love and excitement, and something else. Her little face turned to her father, then back to her mother. Then she spied the suitcase, and all her childish excitement fled. She knew without asking that her little-girl dreams had been shattered.

Mommy wasn't coming home to stay. She was just visiting.

But just the same, she wrapped her little arms around her mother's waist and hugged Jessie tight, as if her heart would break.

Jessie's throat was clogged with a lump as large as a boulder. Her hands came down to hold her child to her. Slowly, she got down on one knee, still holding Amy close. She fit the child's head into the crook of her neck and picked her up, keeping her close as they walked into the house that had once been her home.

Everything that had been said earlier fled her mind. This weekend was precious, and she was going to make the best of it for all of them. There would be no fighting, no cold wars, this weekend. Just the Youngs, as a family, at home. She glanced up just in time to see Philip turn away. His eyes had the glistening of unshed tears. And she realized that he, too, would try hard to make their family close for the weekend.

2

·~ccccccccc·

As far as Jessie was concerned, dinner was a disaster. She didn't care for the housekeeper Philip had chosen no matter how many fantastic letters of recommendation the woman had. But her dislike shouldn't have come as a surprise, since Mrs. Anderson obviously didn't approve of Jessie, either, if her pinched-nosed expression was anything to go by.

Amy chatted gaily through the meal, talking about school and grades and friends, her bright eyes darting from Jessie to Philip and back again, as if she couldn't make up her mind which parent to converse with. Beth sat quietly, the food on her plate barely touched. She smiled every time Jessie smiled at her, but she spoke only when she needed to answer a question directed specifically at her.

Mrs. Anderson, who was in and out all through the meal, quietly but effectively made her presence known by the banging of plates and the clearing of her sinuses.

Jessie had invited the woman to sit at the table with them, but she had given a hard stare and mumbled, "No, thank you," just before she turned her back to Jessie on the pretext of stirring the vegetables. That conversation had ended abruptly and left no doubt as to where the housekeeper's alliances were placed. Philip had wooed and captured another female heart.

"Okay, girls, let's clear the table." Jessie reached for the empty plates, piling them one on top of the other, as they used to do before, when they had been together as a family.

The girls looked at their mother and then to the housekeeper.

"If you don't mind, Mrs. Young, I'd rather do this myself. Little hands just make the work time longer." Mrs. Anderson's voice was stiff with disapproval.

Philip intervened when he saw the light of battle enter Jessie's eyes. "Come on, Jessie. The girls and I want to beat you at Monopoly tonight. You can't always win, you know."

Jessie's voice sounded high and crackling even to her own ears. "I've never played with you before, Philip, only with the girls. I didn't even know you played the game."

Amy skipped around the table and stood at her mother's side, holding out her hand. "Oh, we've been teaching him, Mommy. Only Beth usually wins now," she added with a child's sigh in her voice.

Philip's eyes locked with Jessie's for just a second, but it seemed like a year. "I'm learning, Jessie," he said enigmatically, a second message, this one for her only, conveyed in his words. "Perhaps you can teach me a thing or two." He turned and shrugged. "Who knows? Perhaps I can teach you something, too."

Jessie gripped Amy's hand more tightly than she realized. "I've learned all I want from my self-appointed mentor. Now it's time to put it into practice."

"That ought to be interesting. Just as long as you stick to those things that have proven workable."

"Workable for whom, Philip?" she asked softly as they walked casually toward the living room. "Isn't what's good for a man also good for a woman in today's world?"

"Not necessarily. The sex of the party in question has something to do with life's problems and their solutions."

Her voice deepened as she spoke. "I used to think that, too. Was I wrong!"

Philip answered with a look that spoke volumes. She was reminded of all the other times in their marriage when he had used that look and she had been silenced by it. This time was no different except that she chose not to be goaded by him. She had gotten her point across, and that was all she cared about—for the moment.

"What are you talking about, Mom?" Amy questioned, her face showing her puzzlement as she tried to follow their cryptic conversation.

Jessie glanced at Amy, then Beth, realizing that although the children didn't understand, they knew that something was wrong, and it made them uneasy.

She plastered a smile on her lips. "Okay, kids, let's teach your dad what the game is like when you play for real!"

The children giggled, Philip grinned, and Jessie gave a small sigh of relief. Veiled barbs took a lot out of her.

She was out of practice.

It was after ten o'clock before the children were in bed. Jessie read the girls a story before tucking them in and kissing them good night. She had to hide the tears that threatened to spill over in their presence, knowing that it would only make them apprehensive. They had experienced so much upheaval in their short lives, and it had all been within the past year and a half.

She closed their bedroom door and quietly leaned against it, closing her eyes as the pain of being back home seeped through her body. It was hard, so very hard, to see her own children and know that though they hadn't realized it yet, she was no longer an integral part of their lives.

What had she done by cutting off that portion of her life? The agonizing ache and topsy-turvy confusion in her own muddled mind, along with the death of P.J. and Philip's betrayal, had caused her to run. But was it fair? She didn't know.

In some ways, it was as if she hadn't been gone the past three months. She was just as confused and hurt just as much as ever. What had happened to that woman who held down a responsible job, who had been promoted to assistant manager? Where had the logical thought patterns she had been priding herself on gone to? She slowly walked to the staircase, her mind filled with unanswered questions. She had to shelve them in the back of her mind for another time. Right now she had to check on arrangements for the party the next night. . . .

"Jessie?"

Philip stood at the foot of the stairs. His blond head was tilted up at an angle as he watched her hesitate on the landing. He looked so much like P.J. when he would come bounding up the stairs, yelling at the top of his voice, "Mom, the girls got into my baseball cards again! Will you tell them to stay out of my room?"

A sob caught in her throat, and she turned and ran. She didn't realize that out of habit she was running into the only room in the house that she didn't want to see again—their bedroom. She slammed the door and threw herself across the bed, her shoulders moving with the sobs that came without restraint.

The mattress gave as Philip came to lie beside her. "Hush, darling, hush." His mouth caressed the nape of her neck. His hands were on her shoulders, soothing, stroking, touching her with tenderness as he tried to erase the hurt she was suffering.

Slowly, the sobs subsided, and she turned, vainly attempting to wipe the tears away. Her eyes were probably swollen, her face blotched. She didn't know why she cared that Philip should see her like that, but she did. She kept her eyes downcast.

"I'm sorry."

"So am I. Did one of the girls say something to upset you?"

"No. It was you." She sniffed, uncaring that she had allowed her guard to crumble. The ache in her breast was all she could cope with at the moment. "For a minute, I could see P.J. and . . . and I ran."

"I know. I see him everywhere, too."

She stared up at him. "You? But how?"

"Every time I play with the girls, I'm reminded of how I couldn't make it to one of his baseball games. Every time I work late, I remember how he used to greet me at the door and how I couldn't take the time to listen to him because I wanted to go into the study, have a drink and lick my own wounds," he answered softly, slowly, choosing to bare his soul and show the intensity of the guilt he felt. He was leaving himself vulnerable to her, and they both realized it.

Instead of attacking, she raised one hand and smoothed an errant lock of blond hair from his forehead. "Poor Philip. You're human, too."

He clasped her hand in the warmth of his, bringing it to his cheek to slide along his jawline. "Yes" was his simple answer.

He could have said so many things then. He

could have accused her of leaving him in his time of need. He could have screamed at her for running away when the family needed her most. He could have brought up all the things that had been left unsaid between them, finishing with the heartache they had given each other. But he said none of them, and it was Jessie's undoing.

Without being cognizant of it, Jessie lifted her head off the bed and gently grazed his lips in comfort. With the reality of touching him came an emotion she hadn't felt in a long time—desire. Her other hand circled his neck and pulled him toward her, bringing the strong length of his body into intimate contact with hers. He stiffened, then relaxed, as if he needed her touch as much as she needed his, as if he could no longer fight the inner battle against touching and holding her. His mouth molded itself to hers, his hands tightening their hold on her shoulders as a deep and almost angry hunger communicated itself from him to her. His body forced her back, his passion almost bruising in its intensity.

Memories of other, wonderful times swept through Jessie, and she knew that he felt them, too. Magic formed between them, ordering limbs and torsos to engage in the age-old act of love without a thought to future recriminations.

Her fingers fumbled with the knot in his tie, pulling it almost frenziedly. She needed to touch him, his hair-roughened chest and hardened muscles. She craved the contact and could taste the sweetness of his kisses.

Philip broke the kiss and pressed his lips against

her throat. His breath was feverishly hot on the pulse point in her neck. "Don't do this because you feel sorry for me, Jessie. I don't want your pity."

"Will you pity me if I tell you I need you?" She spoke softly, giving more of herself away than she would have if there had been room for thought. But thoughts had fled, and only heightened, daring emotions reigned.

A groan was forced from his throat as he jerked the tie over his head and helped her to open the front of his shirt. "No, Jessie, no. We need each other. We need this."

Incapable of answering, Jessie held him closer, afraid to let him go in case he pulled away and left her yearning for something that shouldn't be. When he did pull away, a moan rose from deep in her throat, but his kiss once more silenced it. He had resettled himself beside her so that he could reach out and lovingly stroke her from her breast down her side to the slight swell between her thighs, his fingers burning wherever they touched. Possessively, he sought and found the secret to her womanliness, sending shivers down both their spines with the intimate contact.

"I love that about you, Jessie," he murmured into her parted mouth. "You were always ready for me. Always. Do you know how good that made me feel? I could conquer mountains with you in my arms."

His kiss stopped all the breath in her lungs from escaping. How could she even dream of escaping him when his touch was so magical? She could feel the pounding of her heart against the trembling palm of his other hand, intensifying its already rapid beat.

The room was dark, and they undressed each other in seconds, neither willing to lose contact with the other. Jessie's hand trailed down the slim, taut side of his body, then back up the other side, as if reassuring herself that everything was the same. Nothing had changed; no scars had emerged; his strength and desire were still overpowering. A sheen of dampness covered his skin like a suit, telling her that he was as overcome by their love-making as she was, and the knowledge was heady.

His slightly rough tongue traveled a route it had blazed often over the years, heating her to a passion that barely cooled even when he left that spot to tease another. His mouth did crazy things that made her move her tensed and waiting body to help accommodate his wanderings. Their excited breathing filled the silent room, accompanied only by the sounds their bodies made moving against the heavy cotton of the bedspread.

"Here, Jessie. Please," he whispered into the darkness. "Touch me here."

"Only if you'll do the same," she whispered in return, a lightness in her voice that made her sound as if she were floating. "Here." And she took his hand to show him her needs. His lips followed his hands, his body shifting, moving, sliding over hers as he showed her just how much they belonged that way, together.

They were starving, and a feast was offered.

Jessie gorged herself with him. The taste, feel and smell of him were the only food she needed.

He took her hands in his, holding them above her head so she would stop her teasing. "In a minute, darling." His voice was low and chuckling. "Give me one more minute."

She wriggled under his admonishment. "Philip, please."

"Wait. I want to touch you without exploding from the feeling. I need you so much, Jess. So much."

"Please," she murmured, moving as his hand touched the core of her. He teased and taunted, making her arch to his body with her need of him. Finally, he let her go, but not before she was filled with fire for him. Still he continued to seek those pleasure points he knew so well.

When she could finally take no more of his teasing mouth, her hands pulled him to her, and he entered, bringing a sigh of wonder from her lips as they were covered once more by his.

The agony of need turned into the intense pleasure of fulfillment, and she cried out with the release of so many long-denied emotions.

Once more, he hushed her, the tone of his voice soothing her jangled nerves. Still moving softly within her, he reached his own echo of heaven. When he stiffened, she held him close, caressing him with tender hands, speaking to him in soft, soothing murmurs.

They lay in each other's arms in the darkness of the room that held so many memories of past lovings. A tear slid down Jessie's cheek and was absorbed by the pillow beneath her head. She wasn't sure if she was crying because of their actions that night or because of the memories that made her long for what should have been.

The early-morning sky was light outside the curtained windows. Jessie moaned, then turned to bury her head in the pillow and shut out the sounds of movement below. She needed more sleep!

"Wake up, Mommy." Amy's voice was just above a squeak as Beth opened the door to allow her sister to enter. Amy carried a small tray laden with coffee and toast and a small bunch of wildflowers. Both girls had smiles that made Jessie's heart break with their beauty.

Jessie scooted up in bed and smoothed the covers so the tray could be placed in her lap. "My goodness! I certainly didn't expect this!" she exclaimed, picking up the flowers and taking a whiff of their slightly pungent aroma before sipping the almost-cold coffee. "Mmmmm, delicious."

Amy climbed on one side, while Beth sat primly on the other. "Mrs. Anderson made the coffee, but Beth made the toast, and I decorated the tray," she said proudly. "When you lift the saucer up, you'll find a message from us."

Jessie obediently did as she was told. A large square sheet of paper was folded neatly underneath. She opened it, only to have her eyes film over in tears. Flowers decorated the border, while a picture of Amy, Beth, Philip and her was at the top, all of them holding hands. The words blurred as she read, "We love you. Please stay."

She glanced from one to the other, her mouth too dry to form the words that needed to be said. They waited expectantly, Amy excited with hope and Beth trying not to show her fear of refusal.

"Oh, darlings," she began, choking on her own words. What could she possibly say?

"Is there a party going on?" Philip asked from the doorway, and all eyes turned toward him. He was lounging against the doorjamb, arms crossed as he watched the family scene before him. He looked so brave, so confident, so very, very male. Jessie swallowed. His eyes took in the lost expression on Jessie's face before he looked at the children and grinned. "Aren't I invited?"

Amy scooted off the bed and ran past her father. "I'll get you a cup of coffee, too, Daddy. Wait here!" she said as she ran lightly down the steps. Beth remained where she was, trying hard not to show any emotion other than a small, sad smile.

Philip pulled away from the door and sauntered into the room, smiling but cautious. He ruffled Beth's hair.

"And how's my biggest girl doing this morning? I thought you'd be watching cartoons."

"We decided to surprise Mommy with breakfast in bed," she answered shyly, combing her hair with her fingers.

Philip looked at Jessie again. "And were you surprised?"

Jessie swallowed, thankful for his presence. It

gave her time to pull her emotions back into some semblance of order.

"Yes," she murmured, holding out the note the girls had given her.

He took it, read it and then glanced at Beth. "This looks like your handwriting, Beth. You're doing very well," he praised, and her smile shone like a beacon.

Jessie glanced down at the note in his hand. She hadn't realized that Beth had written it. She had thought that she kept in such close contact with the girls, but they had grown without her knowing it. She didn't even recognize her child's handwriting anymore. Her heart dropped to her toes. What else didn't she know about her own children?

Amy concentrated on the coffee cup in her small hands as she carefully walked across the room. "Here, Daddy, I only spilled a few drops."

Jessie watched in silence as Amy wriggled her way onto the bed beside her father, glancing at him warmly when he smiled at her. They had built a bond together, father and children, and it was hard not to see their glowing love.

Suddenly, Jessie felt as if she were the outsider, the interloper, and she cried inside because she knew she had done it to herself. She had left them to seek her place in life, and they had built another life for themselves, one that didn't include her except in the broadest sense of the word. No, that wasn't true. They had done what they had to do, and that was to function without her. She was the one who had discarded them, not the other way around.

The children soon left to watch television, and Philip and Jessie were alone. The muffled noises the girls made drifted up the stairs to them but didn't interfere with the intimacy of the moment.

Philip still sat on the edge of the bed, an arm's length away. His golden-brown eyes carefully scanned her face, checking to see her mood of the moment.

"It's nice finding you here in our bed again." His voice was low and soothing and intimate. His eyes warmed her flesh.

"It feels strange to wake up here," she answered huskily. "I'm used to that small apartment and a much smaller bed."

"You don't have to be there, you know." He hesitated a moment before taking a deep breath. "I want you back, the children want you back, and I think deep down inside you want to come back."

"If you're talking about last night—" she began, only to have him interrupt her.

"I won't make apologies for last night, and I won't listen to any from you. Last night we needed each other and found solace in that need. We should have done it months ago, sharing our needs and fears instead of hiding them from each other."

"I wasn't going to apologize!" she exclaimed heatedly. "I was going to say that last night didn't solve anything. We're still the same two people with the same problems, and going to bed didn't end those problems."

"No, but it helped break down a few of the barriers that we had erected. It's a start."

His hand came out and stroked the hair away from the side of her face, and she immediately reacted to his gentle touch, her face showing her vulnerability.

"And I'd like to make love to you again. Now." His voice was husky with desire. "Would you let me, Jessie? You felt so good in my arms. I needed you." His mouth came closer, teasing hers with a light brush of his lips as his hand moved to stroke her throat softly. "I need you again now."

"Like you needed me all those other years, Philip? As soon as you had your fill, you turned away and went on with your business. I can't go through that again. I won't just be here when you need me and put in a closet when you have other, more important things to do."

"I've never said I thought of you like that." His voice was harsh. His hand dropped from her throat.

"I know you didn't say it. For all I know, you never felt that way. That's not important. Your actions led me to believe that you felt that way." Her hands were clasped in her lap, just below the tray. It might as well be said now, because if he touched her again, she knew she'd forget the words and the emotions that had led to her flight. "You made me feel that I was just someone who was supposed to be here for your benefit and convenience, and it was only when I tried to assert myself that I received any attention from you other than for sex. When I finally succumbed and became the housewife and mother you wanted, I didn't get any attention because I was running smoothly. I wasn't

important anymore. I needed preventive mainte-
nance, but you always greased the squeaky wheels
but ignored the rest as long as there was no
problem."

"That's normal, isn't it?" Philip moved, getting
off the bed and walking toward the window to gaze
outside, his back toward her. "How often did you
praise the children for a good grade or me for a
good brief?" He laughed mirthlessly. "But you
were sure on us if I didn't bring home the right pay
check for braces or the girls didn't do as well in
school as you'd expected. We were like trophies for
you. If we got dusty, we got your attention. As long
as we shone, then you could continue to go your
merry way." He turned to stare at her with hard
eyes. "Isn't that so?"

"It's not the same," she whispered, knowing she
was lying. He was right.

A look of disgust crossed his face. "I might have
done what you accuse me of; I don't know. All I
know is that I loved and trusted you, and you left
me and the children for some damn reason I still
don't understand!" His hand ranged through his
blond hair, ruffling it, and she wanted to reach out
and soothe him once more. She had to get away
from him!

Jessie placed the tray on the side of the bed and
stepped out. Philip had brought her suitcase up
while she slept, and she reached inside for her robe
so she could cover herself quickly. She knew that
Philip was watching her, and a part of her mind was
proud of her new-found figure.

"You're too thin," he pronounced, taking away the pride she had tried so hard to cultivate.

"Not thin enough," she said, facing him with her hands on her hips. "Not smart enough, not sexy enough, not good enough."

"Is there another man?" His body grew stiff with tension. She could feel it from across the room.

"Women don't have to go from one man to another. I don't need to be taken care of, Philip. There is no other man. I just don't happen to want your brand of love."

He strode to her side, and his hands came down hard on her shoulders. His face was a mask of brilliant anger and deep frustration. "But you want me, all right. Just as much as I want you. You're just too damn stubborn to let me know with words. You show it with every move, every nuance."

His lips came down to cover hers in a punishing kiss. His arms circled her back and brought her closer to his tall, lean body, forcing her to acknowledge his great strength and need. She knew better than to resist and bring forth more anger than she could cope with. She stood still as he plundered her mouth and body for a response.

Suddenly, he raised his head. "Damn you for not admitting to yourself that you want me! Damn you!"

He stalked from the room, slamming the door behind him in his anger.

Jessie covered her ears at the noise. She stood on the spot where he had left her, her mind whirling in confusion. Was he right? Had it been as much her fault as it had been his? Was it the lack of communication that had torn them apart and not another woman or P.J.'s death? She didn't know and couldn't think straight anymore. She thought of all the other things she had silently accused him of, all the thoughts that had drifted through her mind in her lonely apartment at night. She had had plenty of time to think during the past three months, but without feedback, without someone else's thoughts, she had stagnated in her opinions.

Maybe they should have had this talk long before now.

But the pain she had suffered fifteen months before had been too deep then even to talk about. She had walked around holding it in, as if exposing it would have poisoned everyone.

She glanced toward the bed, seeing the note the girls had given her again. Once more, her eyes filmed over with tears. Deep inside, she knew they needed her. Probably now more than ever. But they had managed without her, learning to rely on Philip for the things she used to do for them. Could she work her way back into the family again? And if she could, did she really want to do it, knowing that she might have to give up certain things, or did she just want everything?

Questions popped in and out of her head with no sense of order. She couldn't think straight. She stared at the note, attempting to focus on the childish handwriting.

This weekend was the first of many major changes in her life. She could feel it. What she didn't know was what the changes were going to be and how they would affect her, her children, her job—even her husband.

She would just have to wait and see.

3

~~~~~~~~~~~~~~~

Jessie's hands were clammy, her stomach filled with tremors that refused to be calmed. She stared into the mirror as if looking at a stranger. Her golden-red hair had been cut closely to shape her head like a shining cap. It gleamed like a flame under the overhead light in the bedroom. Her makeup was new, and her application of it was dramatic: jewel-green eye shadow in two blending colors, smoky gray mascara and a deep green eye liner defining her already large eyes.

The gown she had chosen for the party was also a rich jewel green, and its silky fabric clung to her new slim form. Just six months earlier it would have shown bulges in some places and revealed fat in others. She took a deep breath, then looked again. This was a new Jessie Young, one that Philip and his parents hadn't really seen before. Tilting her head to see herself in the mirror, she smiled as if she were talking to someone. Even when she had first met Philip, she hadn't looked as good! Why, then, was she shaking with nerves?

She knew the reason. That night she was going to show herself off physically, but those present might be judging her on her mental health and attitude, as well. She might not make the grade either way, and she was scared.

Just after P.J. had died, Philip had sent her to see a psychiatrist to try to talk out her deep depression. Session after session had passed in a vague procession. She cried, and he consoled. But after a year, she remembered only a few of his words out of all those visits. One small remnant of advice seemed pertinent.

"In order to be happy with anyone else, Jessie, you first have to be happy with yourself. The rest will come."

She hoped he had known what he was talking about! Finally learning that she was worth something wasn't an easy thing to do, and every day her value fluctuated.

Once more, Jessie gave a critical glance in the mirror. If she didn't wow them that night, she never would. Now all she had to worry about was conversing with people who were Philip's friends, not hers.

The bedroom door opened, and Amy and Beth stood there, mouths open.

"Mom, you look like a movie star!" Beth whispered, for once speaking before her younger sister.

Jessie turned around, allowing the slightly flared skirt to billow. "You like?"

She chuckled at their stunned looks. Every weekend she had worn comfortable jeans and loose shirts, not bothering to dress up to be with the girls. It was the first they had seen of her transformation.

"Isn't the neckline a little daring?" Philip came and stood behind the children, scowling in disapproval.

She had to force herself to stop staring at him and look back at the children. He was wearing a dark brown three-piece suit and looked every inch a movie star himself. His golden blond hair feathered away from his beautifully etched features. His jaw, football-muscled neck and strong, broad shoulders proclaimed him eminently attractive to even the least susceptible of the female sex. He was simply too handsome to look at without drooling. Damn him! Suddenly, she felt plump and short and inadequate again.

She twirled toward the mirror and pretended to check an earring. "Do you think so?" she inquired lightly. "I think it's just right."

"If anyone stands too close to you—" His voice stopped in his throat with a growl. Both the children and Jessie stared at him in surprise. He was jealous! Philip was jealous of her!

An overwhelming feeling of power exploded away the tension in her stomach. All her married life people had looked at Philip in admiration and then at her as if they wondered what sort of undisclosed dynamic personality she possessed to keep him at her side. For once, she felt that the tables were turned. Now it was his turn to be unsure for a change!

She laughed gaily, sending a provocative glance at him from beneath her sooty lashes. "If anyone comes too close to me, they'll catch a whiff of my new perfume, 'Danger,'" she teased. She amazed herself. She was flirting with him! What had gotten into her?

His pale brown eyes hardened. His answer was to turn on his heel and leave, his hollow footsteps echoing down the stairs and toward the living room.

The slightly strained smile on Jessie's face remained as she helped the girls into their party clothes. They would watch TV upstairs, then join the guests for a little while before she tucked them into their beds and kissed them good night. Perhaps he wasn't jealous. Perhaps he was right and she was making a fool of herself in that dress. Perhaps everyone would laugh at her or be shocked at her lack of decorum. Perhaps . . . The doorbell sounded, and Jessie realized that she had no choice in the matter now. She'd have to face their guests in what she was wearing and take the chance that her mirror and her taste in clothing were right.

Pretending to smile as her in-laws were ushered through the door, she said a quick prayer and began the long descent down the staircase.

Helen Young was tall, slender and every inch a lady. Her dark brown hair had turned slightly copper colored over the years, and the wrinkles around her eyes were more pronounced, but her carriage was that of visiting royalty. It was odd that such a cool exterior held such a warm nature, but it did. John, her husband, was an older rendition of Philip, his blond hair streaked with gray. Slightly overbearing for Jessie's taste, he always knew his mind and confidently spoke his personal opinions in a louder voice than was necessary. But in his own way he was nice, too.

"Jessie?" John's voice boomed in the entryway. "My God, girl! I wouldn't have recognized you on the street! You look fantastic!"

Jessie dimpled this time, her smile sincere. As she took the last stair, she held out her hands to him, giving his a squeeze. "It's good to see you again, John, and I'll hold your words close to my heart. Not many people know that I've finally emerged from my slightly chubby cocoon." She gave his cheek a kiss before turning to Helen and doing the same.

"It's good to see you again, Jessie." Helen spoke in a quiet voice, but her eyes showed that she wasn't just being polite; she meant what she said.

"Thank you," Jessie said softly, tucking her arm through the older woman's and leading her away from the hall stairs. "Philip?" Her glance bounced off him, reluctant to be caught by his piercing eyes. He stood tall and straight in the arched entryway of the living room. "How about some drinks?"

He walked to the bar and poured his father and himself straight shots of scotch after giving his mother and Jessie glasses of wine. The silence was stilted.

Jessie spoke first, attempting to cover her nervousness. "The bartender had a flat and called to say he'd be late. He shouldn't be too much longer."

"Good." Helen took Jessie's hand and guided her over to the couch. "Now you and I have a little time to talk before the guests arrive." She sat down, slipping off her black pumps before turning to Jessie. "I'm so glad you're here to help us celebrate. I was hoping you'd accept. What have you been doing with yourself"—she chuckled—"besides breaking out of your shell to become a most delightfully beautiful woman?"

Jessie shrugged, her glance wandering over to Philip and his father as they discussed a court case. "Nothing much. I'm assistant manager in a dress shop, and most of my energy is gone by the end of the day."

"Meanwhile, you dieted and changed your hair and makeup." Helen looked at Jessie closely, her eyes gentle. "Somehow I get the feeling that the new you is all on the outside and the old you is still there, inside." She forced Jessie to look at her. "Am I right?"

"Does it show?"

Helen patted her hand. "It doesn't," she said reassuringly. "I just know what it's like to go through that metamorphosis and still be the same inside."

Jessie vaguely remembered Helen saying once before that it had taken her years to change from the gangling goose of her youth to the swan people knew her as today. For one frightening moment, she had thought that Helen had been hinting at her relationship with Philip, and her heartbeat had stilled. Helen didn't know most of the reasons for their separation, and Jessie didn't want to be the one to explain. It was better not discussed, even better not thought of.

Helen smiled her gentle understanding of the conflicts going on inside Jessie. "No one really changes on the inside, Jessie; they only learn to see things differently as they grow older."

The doorbell rang, and the guests began arriving. Slightly raised brows and overly friendly smiles were aimed Jessie's way. A few of the couples didn't even bother to hide their shock at her "new" appearance.

"My dear, you've lost a great deal of weight. No man is worth losing your looks for, you know," one woman muttered conspiratorily into Jessie's ear. Jessie didn't mention that the woman's husband had a definitely lecherous gleam in his eye as he mentally undressed her slim but still-curved figure. After a little while, Jessie was able to extricate herself from the couple. Smiling stiffly, she excused herself to put Beth and Amy to bed and check on the staff in the kitchen.

As she walked across the room, she could feel eyes boring into her, making her aware of every step she took. When she reached the hallway, she glanced over her shoulder to discover the person who was watching her so closely. Philip stood in front of the fireplace with a small group of men. He was obviously listening to the conversation, but his light brown eyes were searing her skin and making it prickle. She rounded up the girls and left the room quickly, needing time to make her body respond to her own demands and not his unspoken ones. But the sensation he had caused continued to react on her already-tensed nerves.

When she entered the kitchen twenty minutes later, it was organized bedlam. Three women had been hired to help serve, and their busy hands filled silver and crystal trays with delicious tidbits. Mrs. Anderson stood by the oven, popping out hot hors d'oeuvres and handing them to the next in line.

"Do you need any help?" Jessie smiled, receiving in return a smile from everyone except Mrs. Anderson.

"Why? Isn't there enough food out there?" the housekeeper retorted.

"The food is fine. I just thought I'd lend a hand."

Philip walked in to stand beside her, his hand tightening on her waist. "Mrs. Anderson has everything under control. Come and help me make an anniversary toast to mom and dad." He smiled at the women and then guided Jessie out the door. She had no choice but to follow; his grip was almost painful.

When they reached the hallway, Philip turned toward her in the soft darkness. "Jessie," he said tightly, then gave a moan of impatience before turning and shoving her into the small half bath off the hall.

"Philip!" she protested halfheartedly, but his lips came down and stopped anything she might have said. The room was pitch black, the space confining. Philip's hand unerringly found and locked the small door before pulling her to him once more.

But Jessie didn't notice as her traitorous body succumbed to his nearness and her arms twined around his neck.

He leaned against the sink, taking her weight with him as his hands plundered her body from soft breasts to tender thighs. "My God, you're driving me crazy!" he muttered, continuing to kiss her throat, her hair, the soft underside of her chin, his lips awakening a heightened response by not kissing her on the mouth again.

"You've been teasing me all night, twitching that delightful bottom as you snare every man's attention, flirting with everyone but me. You wouldn't even smile my way until you met me in the crowd face to face. And then you throw a provocative glance over your shoulder and leave the room! Just how much do you think I can take?"

"But you said I was too skinny." Her lips tried to find his. Still he teased, not allowing himself to be captured.

"You damn well know you aren't," he growled. "I liked you better the other way. You were mine then, and I didn't have to fend off others to get to you."

"You said my hair was too short."

"It's easier to kiss your neck and shoulders this way," he mumbled, his lips trailing a path over the area he had just discussed. "My God, Jessie . . ."

Jessie's hands left his neck and held each side of his strong jaw tenderly, her fingers trembling with reaction. "Don't talk. Hold me, kiss me. Please," she whispered softly into his mouth.

A small moan echoed inside her before he crushed her to him, his hands pulling her toward him so tightly that she thought she might disappear inside him. And that was where she wanted to be.

No! Thoughts screamed in her head. You want independence! A life of your own! But she wanted Philip more. Was there no such thing as happiness? Was there only this fleeting feeling of ecstasy, the rest all discontent and drivel?

Philip's mouth lowered to her breast, brushing the offending material of her gown aside so he could tease one dusky nipple with his tongue. Jessie arched to him, not wanting the delicious feeling to stop. Not wanting Philip to stop. He had never been as hungry for her before, and the feeling was headier than the most potent wine.

He slipped down the other strap of her gown, his mouth moving toward its new goal. "The other," he muttered. "I want both. I want it all."

Her breath stopped in her throat at his words. She cradled his head with her hands, her own head resting on top of his as he tortured her with his expertise. Her hands slowly trailed down his neck and shoulders to cup his hips, one hand trailing along his zipper to feel his need.

"Don't." His hand covered hers, slowly bringing it back up to his chest as he gasped for breath. "The show will be over before it's begun."

He stopped his pillaging and held her close, placing her head next to the beating of his heart. One hand rested on her breast as if it were the most important contact in the world, while the other rested lightly on her hip. They quieted together, each realizing that they had to go out and face their guests.

"Damn," he muttered, a rueful note in his voice that made Jessie smile. "I wish we were at someone else's party so we could leave."

A noise outside the door startled them both into silence. Jessie held her breath as the intruder tried the locked door before turning away. "Someone must be in there. I'll check upstairs. There's probably another one there." The woman's voice drifted off as she walked up the stairway.

"We've got to get out, which may be much trickier than coming in." Jessie chuckled.

"It's okay for you to laugh, but what would my clients think of me coming out of a bathroom in this shape . . . holding my wife's hand?" he teased back, finishing his sentence before he felt her stiffen in his arms. "Jessie," he tried to explain, but she refused to listen.

"It would be so much more acceptable if you were with someone else, wouldn't it, Philip? More macho and far more titillating."

She reached for the door, unlocking it swiftly before opening it. "Thanks for the interlude."

The light from the dim hallway was enough to allow her to see his grim expression. But she couldn't stop her words or actions. She tilted her head to one side as if studying him. "You know, maybe that's what we're both best at: a taste of danger; illicit love."

Her steps were quick as she walked down the hall and up the stairs, unable to take a breath until she reached the landing. It was going to take some time to get herself back together. Mentally, she might never achieve it, but physically she needed the help of cosmetics and time by herself.

". . . you haven't seen her yet? Well, you're in for a treat! She's lost so much weight, and her hair is cut in such a becoming style. I'm sure she'll be pleased to see you, too." Jessie could make out the voice of one of Helen's close friends. "Did Jessie know you were coming tonight?"

Jessie stood at the entrance to her bedroom, her face showing her surprise. Was that who had tried the bathroom?

"Dianna?" she said, and as the dark-haired woman turned around to confirm her thoughts, Jessie opened her arms to return the hug. "I had no idea! Phil didn't say a word!" she cried excitedly. She held Dianna Weston's hands in her own, more for emotional support than any other reason. "You look terrific!" Jessie eyed the other woman's figure, slim and yet more filled out than usual. Her dark hair was coiled on top of her head, her eyes a peaceful, serene hazel.

"And having another baby seems to agree with you," Jessie teased. "You're what, almost five months pregnant—again?" she asked, and Dianna grinned, nodding her answer. They nodded their excuses to Helen's friend, then walked over to the bed, both of them sitting down so they could talk without the others overhearing.

"With two children in almost two years, I'd better say that pregnancy is wonderful, but nothing can beat the finished product *not* kicking your ribs black and blue!" Dianna chuckled. "Noah says that this time we're having a boy. He doesn't like the feeling of being outnumbered. Goodness knows why, with Tabby and Honey drooling all over his manly form!" She chuckled, her eyes lighting with happy memories. "But I don't pay too much attention to his ramblings; he's always got a silly grin on his face!"

Philip had been the attorney for Noah Weston's computer firm and other ventures, including the recording company, until Noah had sold most of his businesses to a conglomerate. Now Noah, though still in his late thirties, was semiretired, while Philip continued to manage his other, smaller businesses.

"I'll just bet he is. I told you once that Noah was a pushover for a pretty face, especially yours." Jessie didn't have to mention that Catherine Sinclair had tried to ruin both their marriages. Dianna had fought back—and won.

"So you did," Dianna said softly, a small smile turning up the corners of her mouth. "But what have you been doing? I haven't heard from you in months!"

"I'm living in the same apartment and working at the same store. Last month I was promoted to assistant manager, and I'm hoping that someone higher up will notice my skill and handling of unusual circumstances and say, 'Hey, that girl should be a manager!' But so far, nothing." Jessie shrugged, looking down at her hands. She was still shaking slightly from her encounter with Philip. But no matter how hard she tried not to think of him, she knew that after the company left that night, she was going to make love to him, there, on that bed. She knew it. Dianna interrupted her thoughts.

"And what about you and Philip? Does your presence here tonight mean that you two are getting back together?" Her eyes showed the depth of the concern she felt, and Jessie reached out to pat her hand and reassure her that she was all right.

"No, it means that I'm visiting." She gave a trembling sigh. "I thought I knew what I was doing when I walked in the door yesterday, but right now I'm not too sure. I feel as if I've gone back in time, and I'm as confused as ever." Dianna was the only person she could say that to. No one else had ever become close to Jessie, and no one else knew of the reasons behind Jessie's marital situation except Dianna. It felt good to say the words that had been bottled up inside her.

"Is there someone else for you?" Dianna's voice was soft.

"No," Jessie answered. "Oh, my boss takes me out for coffee or dinner occasionally, but it's strictly business." She didn't mention his kind words or the sparkle in his eyes.

"Then why not go through the rest of your metamorphosis at home with Philip and the family? He hasn't been the same since you left him, you know."

"You've seen him?" Philip hadn't mentioned seeing Dianna since Jessie had left.

"Yes, he's come to the ranch several weekends when you've had the children. He's terribly lonely and even more heartbroken than we realized."

"I'm surprised he hasn't had someone with him to ease his 'loneliness.'" Jessie looked at her friend from beneath her lashes. "Hasn't he spoken of his treasure of a secretary? She hangs all over his every word."

"So what?" Dianna raised a brow, daring Jessie to say more.

"Well, he could always find solace with her."

"Jealous?"

"You're damn right I am! Philip's supposed to be mine, yet every woman he runs into pants all over him as if he's the only ram in a valley of ewes! And he doesn't seem to mind it much." Her voice was laced with contempt.

"And you're not going to compete for his affections," Dianna finished for her.

"No."

"Then why lose the weight? Philip always liked you the way you were. And why change the hair and makeup? I don't mean they don't look great on you; you know they do. But did you do all that just for yourself? Did you do it for another man? Or did you"—Dianna hesitated, her hazel-eyed gaze not straying from Jessie—"do it because you wanted Philip to realize just how much he missed by not coming up to the mark?"

Jessie smiled ruefully. "You see an awful lot, don't you?"

Dianna grinned. "Only enough for my mouth to get the rest of me into trouble," she said. "But I am going to give you a piece of advice a very wise woman once gave me. Give Philip time and a chance to understand you. I guarantee it's worth it."

"I must have had a fever when I said that," Jessie muttered, but a small smile played over her lips. "Besides, I've already taken my own advice. I'm trying to talk to him about me, but, well . . ." She hesitated.

"But you're still talking about abstracts and things that happened in the past," Dianna finished.

Footsteps thumped on the stairs. "Dianna?" Noah's deep voice echoed in the upper hall.

Dianna's face lit up at the sound of her husband's approach. "I'm here, darling." She gave Jessie's hand a squeeze and stood; she was walking toward the door when Noah appeared.

"I knew you had to be with Jessie. You two could always talk each other's ears off." He grinned, his glance tender and playful as he looked lovingly at his wife before smiling a greeting to Jessie. "Philip was worried about you. He said he didn't know where you had disappeared to, but I told him I could track you down."

Jessie walked over and gave his cheek a kiss. "I'd better get back down there and play hostess before everyone disappears." She started out the door, then turned. "But you two had better stay long enough for me to have a nightcap with you!" she ordered, then left, unable to watch Noah take Dianna in his arms for a quick, secluded kiss.

"Where have you been?" Philip growled, staring at her with icy golden eyes. "Everyone thought we had a fight and you left again."

"Sorry to put you in such an embarrassing position." Jessie's voice was stiff. "I was talking to Dianna."

"Well, for heaven's sake, do your talking later! You're supposed to be the hostess tonight. Remember? We were going to toast my parents half an hour ago!"

"We couldn't. I was maneuvered against my will into a dark hall bathroom for a quick feel and a stolen kiss half an hour ago. Do you remember?" She turned and walked away, her anger just barely under control. How dare he scold her? She was a grown woman and could do what she wanted! No one chastised him for not mingling when he stood at the fireplace and exchanged jokes with the men!

Philip didn't leave her side for the rest of the evening. Was he checking to make sure she mingled properly? Just the very idea made her temper simmer again. They toasted Helen and John and exchanged conversation with their acquaintances. The drinks and food disappeared, the mess cleaned up as they went. Everything was going smoothly despite Jessie's feelings of anger.

But aside from her anger, her topsy-turvy emotions were competing with the logical advice that Dianna had given earlier. Give Philip time. Did she still love him enough to do that? She knew she did. The truth was that she was afraid of his getting to know her innermost thoughts, then rejecting her for them, so she had made offense her own best defense. Why had it taken so long for her to figure that out? She didn't know.

By the end of the evening, Jessie was a bundle of

nerves and totally exhausted. Noah and Dianna stayed to have one last drink with them before heading home, and Jessie made a date to have lunch with her friend later the next week. It would be good to talk to her again. She missed women's conversations. Business didn't allow much time for friendships.

Mrs. Anderson appeared in the shadow of the hallway as they were saying good night to Philip's parents. Jessie's stomach felt slightly squeamish, and her head was beginning to throb heavily with the beat of her heart. It would be wonderful to get into bed and close her eyes. Sleep was already shrouding her brain in cotton, and all thoughts of making love with Philip had disappeared amid her anger and exhaustion.

When the door closed, Mrs. Anderson stepped forward. "Everything's picked up and washed. I'm going to retire now. I'll do the dusting and vacuuming tomorrow," she said in her usual monotone.

"Fine, Mrs. Anderson. And thank you for your efficiency. You did a wonderful job." Jessie actually felt grateful to the woman, who had kept on top of the evening's cleaning. At least she hadn't had that worry. Phil was enough of a problem.

"That's just what it was, Mrs. Young," the older woman sniffed. "My job. I often do this when Mr. Young entertains. I'm used to it."

Something snapped in Jessie. She was tired and not feeling well, and Mrs. Anderson was fast becoming a pain! "In that case, I withdraw my compliment." Jessie turned and walked up the stairs, leaving a surprised Philip and his housekeeper in the hallway to discuss the arrangements for the next day.

She almost hesitated in the upstairs hallway, wondering if she could eavesdrop on their conversation, then thought better of it. But if she found out later that Philip had apologized to Mrs. Anderson for her behavior, she'd kill him! That woman had been rude to her since Jessie had walked in the door. She crept into the room she had claimed as hers, the guest room, and walked to the bed. Suddenly, her eyes closed, and she could hardly force her hands to unzip her dress. The gown was quickly discarded; her shoes and panty hose littered the floor seconds later. Within a minute, she was between the sheets, too exhausted to move to the center of the bed. Within two minutes, she was asleep, while the night's problems re-enacted themselves in her dreams.

Tomorrow would be soon enough to think out answers to her own private questions. Tomorrow, tomorrow . . .

4

~~~~~~~~~~~

Morning came too quickly. Jessie stirred, then cringed from the bright light streaming in through the window. With a deep moan, she shoved her head under the pillow, only to find a hand there.

She groped to feel it further. It was big, long fingered and hairy wristed—and wearing a narrow watch band. One blue eye peeped open, and she lifted a corner of the pillow. Philip was lying on his side, a small grin on his face, watching as she tried to focus through her pounding headache.

"Good morning." His voice rang loudly in her ear and sent an echoing shudder through her body.

She moaned again, closed her eyes, then opened them once more, hoping it would help to keep him in her line of vision. Was she still dreaming?

"What are you doing here?" she muttered mutinously.

"I'm watching you. I followed you up by five minutes, but you were already out. I didn't think you had that much to drink."

"I didn't. My nervous system just couldn't take any more."

"How are you feeling now?" His hand came out to brush the bright cap of hair away from her squinting eyes but lingered on the nape of her neck.

"As bad as I felt last night. Worse," she confirmed after trying to adjust both eyes to the sunlight streaming over his shoulder and failing miserably. She closed her eyes, waiting for them to slowly adjust to the light.

"I wonder why that is?" he murmured, a hint of laughter in his tone.

"It's because last night you made me angry, frustrated and filled with regret over attending the party." Her voice snapped in the room, and she held her breath as a pain stabbed behind her eyes.

"It's better than feeling nothing, Jessie. And that seems to be the way you've been acting for months."

"On whose authority do you have that?"

"Mine." His voice softened, his eyes showing an understanding she wouldn't have thought him capable of feeling.

"I'm sorry. I didn't mean to attack you so early."

"You were going to wait until later in the day?" he teased gently, his hand still playing with her hair. She liked the soothing motions his fingers made. They miraculously quieted her nerves. She gave a small wry smile, not realizing just how appealing she looked.

"Why are you here, Phil? Why aren't you in your own room, in your own bed?"

"Because you weren't there."

Her voice turned bitter. "Like a good wife should be? Is that what you're trying to say?"

"If I were trying to say that, I would have. I don't have any problem getting my meaning across to others—just to you."

"Meaning that you have to put things in simpler language so I can understand it?" She couldn't still her wayward tongue. It acted entirely on its own and spewed words she could have cried over.

"Meaning that I mean only what I say." His voice turned firm. "Don't put words in my mouth, Jessie. I'll say exactly what I think . . . not what you think I mean."

She sat up, brushing away his hand. "Yes, sir, Mr. Attorney, sir."

Philip sat up, too, his face going from softened smiles to hard and implacable. "Don't barrage me with words that don't mean anything. You do that every time you think I might get too close, Jessie, and I'm tired of it. Talk to me, argue, scream, but say what you feel when you feel it. Otherwise, we'll never resolve our differences."

Jessie was silent, staring at the wall opposite the bed. It held a painting that had fascinated her from the first time she had seen it. It was a picture of a fog-shrouded cliff with a couple standing apart, arms outstretched to each other. The fog surrounded them; the surf below pounded out their words;

the jaggedness of the cliff separated them. Yet the artist had created the feeling that the parted couple wanted nothing more than to be together. They were separated by the elements. She had seen the painting at an art show years earlier and had been struck by the force of the couple's emotions. Had she known deep inside that it was she and Philip? Or had she secretly wanted the gulf between them to widen?

"Jessie?" His voice recalled her from her introspection, making her blush with guilt over not paying attention to his words.

"I . . ." She halted, not sure what to say, and then became confused and said more than she had wanted to. "I think I know what you mean, Phil. But I've tried for so long to be what you want and shield you from that which you never wanted to hear, that it's hard to bare my inner thoughts for your inspection."

"I know" was all he said as he reached out to hold her close to him in an embrace that was meant more to comfort than to create desire. They lay in silence, absorbing each other's thoughts. As each moment passed, Jessie felt his energy flowing through her, healing her, sorting through her chaotic thoughts to make sense at last, giving her peace.

The Young family at home, Jessie mused as she watched Philip tease Amy and Beth into smiles over breakfast. Soon they would all rise and leave for church—together. Instead of feeling that old locked-in panic, it warmed her to think of them together. She refused to dwell on the fact that she would be leaving that afternoon. It was pushed to the back of her mind. Her thoughts fleetingly rested on the one who was absent—P.J.—but the old pain wasn't as sharp as it had been before. There was just a heartfelt sadness that he wasn't sharing the day with them. That would probably never go away. But the girls were there, and Jessie felt lucky to be a part of them.

Only a few eyebrows were raised when Jessie, Philip and the girls entered church and found a pew. And those few she ignored. When they sang one of the girls' favorite hymns, Amy reached up and took her mother's hand, a special smile on her lips as she sang in a clear childish voice. Jessie's heart swelled with love.

They walked out in silence; even the children weren't chattering as they usually did. The car was warm, the December day even warmer. The windows were rolled down to take advantage of the unseasonable temperature, and also to create a cooling breeze. Philip had remembered that Jessie hated using the air conditioner unless it was absolutely necessary. Occasionally, he glanced over at her, his golden-brown eyes caressing her with his easily read thoughts, and she couldn't help but smile in return.

"Are we having roast today, Mom?" Beth had finally found her tongue. "We always used to have roast on Sunday."

"I don't know, darling. Philip?" she asked, wondering if he had information on how the rest of the day was to be spent.

"No roast. We have a picnic waiting for us at the

house. Mrs. Anderson has been packing it since we left. We're going out for the afternoon." Philip grinned at the girls' response, but his eyes were trained on Jessie's reaction.

She vanquished his doubts. "It sounds wonderful. As soon as we get home, girls, change into your jeans and T-shirts. Last one dressed is a rotten egg!"

Philip drove into the garage, and the children piled out, whooping with energy and joy.

As Jessie reached for the door handle, his hand came out to clasp her other hand in his. "Thanks. I think the kids need this as much as we do."

Jessie nodded, afraid her voice would crack if she answered him. What had her confused thoughts and search for independence done to the people she loved so much? It was hard to realize that she could give them joy just by being with them when only a few months ago she had honestly believed in her heart that they wouldn't miss her any more than they would miss a maid. How wrong could one grown woman be?

They drove to the upper part of Lavon Lake, where Philip said he knew of a perfect setting for a picnic. He was right.

Trees lined the banks of the lake, and a deep verdant moss grew in the shadows where grass couldn't. The empty picnic tables told them that they would have no neighboring picnickers. The children immediately began playing Frisbee, laughing with unrestrained joy, while Philip leaned back and watched Jessie unpack the contents of the picnic hamper.

Jessie glanced up to watch the children, only to have her eyes captured by Philip's. Her heart skipped a beat, then began to thump in an erratic pattern as his look totally devoured her. For a few seconds, they were lost in their own world. She forgot all the small, inconsequential arguments, all their problems, as she remembered the many wonderful, exciting events that had brought them together. That feeling of wild expectation at the thought of being in each other's arms hadn't dwindled with time. In fact, if her body's immediate response was anything to go by, she was even more excited by him now than when they had first met.

He smiled lazily, placing his hands behind his head and stretching to show off his broad chest and large biceps. "That's what I like to see. A domesticated wife fitting into her niche," he teased, but his words did more damage than good.

"That's been the problem all along," she snapped, suddenly brought back to the present. Those small arguments had turned into large ones again. "Your view on what role I should play."

The smile was wiped off his face. She could almost feel his muscles tighten in anger, and her own responded in kind.

"If my view was archaic, it was because I was trained as a boy to believe that I should set the pace for the family I nurtured. I didn't do it out of spite or anger but out of love for you and the children. You didn't have to follow my obviously misguided lead all those years."

"I was a victim of the same kind of upbringing,

remember?" She took out a platter of fried chicken and set it on the redwood table. Suddenly, the sun disappeared behind a gray cloud, and she was cold and tired again. She shouldn't have looked forward to the picnic with such great expectations. She should have known that they would end up arguing. They couldn't be alone together for more than a few minutes before the sparks of animosity flew in the air between them, singeing them both with their heat.

"That might be, but you never said no to anything I did. You went blithely along with my views, never quarreling or arguing with me. You're willing to lay all the blame on me for the way we both were raised and how we patterned our marriage, but you never discussed it until after you had packed your bags and left. How was I supposed to know I was playing the tyrant when you always seemed so happy with the way things were?"

Her face flushed at his accusation. Those words were so close to the mark. He had been role playing, but so had she. Any doubts or unhappiness that she might have felt, she had hidden, thinking them unwomanly or unmotherly or unworthy of comment. She couldn't risk being laughed at. It had been as much her fault as his, perhaps even more.

"Talk to me, Jessie. Don't clam up now."

He hadn't laughed at her candor that morning. Perhaps he wouldn't now. "I know I kept my feelings hidden from you so you wouldn't know just how insecure I was. It was all a big bluff on my part, but it didn't seem that way at the time."

As if trying to read her mind, he stared at Jessie, his look searing through her. She ducked her head as she reached for the condiments.

"I didn't know, either, until you left," he answered softly, but with a wealth of understanding. "When you moved out, you took a part of me with you. I had grown complacent in our love, but I wanted more from you, even though I didn't know how to tell you so. We had drifted along that path for so long." He hesitated, leaning forward to rest his arms on his lean legs as his eyes continued to bore into her, telling her more than she was ready to know.

His voice lowered as he shifted forward even more. "I love you, Jessie."

Her heart screamed at his words. He was trying to make her feel guilty for leaving, and he was succeeding. Her face froze in a sterile expression. "I've heard that all my married life. At one time, I even thought I knew what love meant. Now it just sounds like a platitude, something you say to someone else to fill a gap in the conversation."

"But it's true. I love you." The air vibrated with his words; they echoed inside her head over and over. Suddenly, she wanted to cry, to slap him, to accuse him of all the dishonest and ugly things that had happened in the past. But her tongue was stilled by the look of pain on his handsome face.

For the first time, she fully realized that he, too, had suffered from their separation. Oh, she knew it had been hard to get a suitable housekeeper and find a routine for the children, as well as working their activities around his own schedule. But the fact that he had suffered from the loss of her presence astounded her, and she stared at the open pain reflected in his eyes. She shook her head to clear it of her thoughts.

She couldn't have been wrong! There were other women! She knew it!

And that thought hurt her most of all.

Was it pride or a deep sense of loss at what had been that made her look away? She couldn't say. All she knew was that once more she was warring with herself. One part of her wanted to cut him to ribbons with words, while the other part wanted to be safely enfolded in his arms, protected from the outside world and all its problems.

And she couldn't do either.

Both Jessie and Philip dropped the conversation, silently willing each other not to let personal problems spoil the children's picnic. As the afternoon sun dropped beyond the tall pine trees, the children started to droop from exhaustion after all their activity. They sat down to eat a silent meal. Afterward, Jessie played tag with them for a while; then Philip continued the game of Frisbee while she repacked the picnic basket.

Mrs. Anderson had done a marvelous job of catering to their varied tastes, and Jessie was thankful for that, though she wished the housekeeper wouldn't be so cold to her. She wasn't that way with the children, who seemed to love her. Apparently, Mrs. Anderson didn't care for Jessie and had decided to show it in little ways.

It was after dark by the time they got home. Amy went through the house, flipping light switches on as she slowly dragged her feet toward the upstairs bathroom. Jessie followed closely behind, quietly turning off every other one under Philip's austere stare.

The girls bathed and climbed into bed, their smiles showing the depth of their weariness. Jessie kissed them both, read them a story, then kissed them again. She sat in the old rocking chair and watched them tumble into dreamland, not leaving the room until she was certain they were both asleep, and then only reluctantly.

Philip stood in the living room, a drink in his hand as he stared into space. The expression on his face was one of agony, and her heart went out to him.

"Philip?"

He turned, and his mask slipped back into place. After taking a gulp of his drink, he lifted his glass toward her. "Care for one?"

"No, thank you." Jessie continued to stand in the doorway, watching him.

"I guess you're ready to leave."

"Yes."

"Are the children asleep?"

"Yes."

"Good, then there won't be any teary good-bys."

"No," she whispered. "No teary good-bys." She hoped she wouldn't cry or beg to stay. Her pride had received a few hard knocks already that day, and she didn't think she could stand another.

"Where's your carryall?"

"In the hallway."

"Let's go, then. I have some work to do this evening. I'll just tell Mrs. Anderson we're leaving."

The ride back to Jessie's apartment was quiet. Neither spoke, and the small space between them could have been an ocean. They were apart from each other once more, two separate bodies leading two separate lives. But the weekend had changed the impersonal status that they had both tried so hard to maintain. Together they had interacted as a family, as husband and wife and as lovers. Jessie's stomach clenched with the memory of their love-making. It had been more wonderful, more tender, more ecstatic, than she had remembered. Just thinking of his hands on her body, his roughened chest on hers, made her heart beat extra fast.

Philip walked her to her apartment door. "Will you want the girls next weekend, too?" he asked.

"If it's all right with you," she answered.

"That's fine. I'm going out of town for the weekend."

A sharp pain slammed into her middle. Was he going alone, or would there be a woman with him? Would they make love, speak tender words, laugh intimately together? Then she remembered Dianna's words. She had said that Philip had been going to their ranch on weekends. Perhaps . . . ?

"Are you going to the Westons' ranch?" She tried to make her voice sound casual, but even she could hear the tension in it.

"Did Dianna tell you that I've been there?"

"She mentioned it, yes."

"Well, that's not where I'm going this time. I

thought I'd fly to Atlanta and see an old friend." He handed her the key to her opened apartment. His cursory glance was cool, silently telling her that she had forfeited the right to know any personal information concerning him and his activities. "Have a nice week," he said as he turned to go.

"Philip?"

He turned, and suddenly Jessie didn't know what to say. His name had tumbled out in an effort to make him stay. "Good night," she mumbled stiffly, then walked into her apartment and shut the door.

She didn't even bother to turn on the lights as she strained to hear his footsteps on the stairs. When they dwindled away into the night, she felt more empty, more lonely, than she had ever been before. She wanted to fling open the door, run after Philip and call him back. She wanted to hold him in her arms and use him like a talisman to keep away the bad dreams. She wanted to soften under his touch, feel the hardness of his body next to hers. She wanted to melt into the deep inside of him so she would never feel so lonely and helpless again.

Crumbling onto the couch, Jessie cried. Great sobs racked her body as she succumbed to the almost-unbearable grief life had handed her. For the first time since P.J.'s death, Jessie could feel the heartbreaking emotions that she had blocked for so long, and they overwhelmed her. She had shed many tears since that fatal day, but they had been tears of self-pity, and none had assuaged the agony locked inside her as these did.

She saw herself as others saw her, and even though she knew the innermost reasons and emotions that lay behind her actions, she hated the image she conjured up.

Some saw a woman who had left her children and ventured into a new social and business world, as if on a shallow lark. They hadn't known the indecision, the incredible numbness that was in her heart. They didn't see that she had tried to weigh the children's stability over her own selfish feelings of wanting them with her even though it would mean their changing schools and houses. They only saw her callously leaving them.

Others saw a woman who refused to mention her son's name after his death. They didn't see that she couldn't mention him because she would break down completely if she did. He had been her sunshine!

And others saw a frumpy housewife who deserted her handsome, doting husband. They didn't know about Catherine or his good-looking, exciting secretary, who had succeeded in making herself indispensable to him, or the myriad other women in his life, both professionally and socially. They assumed that she had no values, no sense of commitment. They didn't realize that she had wanted his love so badly that she had been stifling without it and that her only way out had been to give him his freedom and regain her own self-respect.

Were her emotional reasons just excuses for doing what she had really wanted to do all along? She didn't know. It was the very first time she had ever confronted herself in a completely honest way, and she wasn't certain of any of the answers.

But at least she had faced the questions. Now, perhaps one at a time, she could answer them.

Her feet dragged as she readied herself for bed. She had to go to work again in the morning, and she had a full schedule. They were opening a new store in a new shopping center, and her boss had asked her to organize a small party for all the employees to help celebrate.

She hoped she'd be able to sleep. A vision of Philip smiling at her as she had awakened that morning filled her senses. After spending the weekend with him, in his bed and in his life, she missed him terribly. Perhaps, if she were careful and took one step at a time, she could walk toward him and into a relationship that would have value and meaning in both their lives.

Perhaps—if he would allow it.

Philip sat in the dark interior of the car, his hand not quite steady enough to start the ignition. His eyes automatically sought the windows of Jessie's apartment. One overhead light was on. No shadows danced on the gleaming windows; no sound came from her apartment. She was in there alone, where she wanted to be.

She didn't want to have anything to do with him; that much was obvious. She had agreed to spend the weekend with him, and now she was probably relieved that it was over. He had forced himself on her at every opportunity, and only after a great deal of coercing had she succumbed to his wishes. He hit the steering wheel in frustration. Had it been for old times' sake? Had he made her feel so guilty that she agreed to have sex with him in order to keep him calm and rational? He'd occasionally acted as if he were out of his mind these past months.

If it were possible, he loved her more now than he had ever loved her during their years together, far more than when he had met and married her over twelve years before. A grim smile turned his lips up.

They had met in college; he had been a senior and she a sophomore. She had always been slightly on the plump side, with sparkling eyes that told of her total enjoyment of life and her intimate knowledge of its funny secrets. She had captivated him at once. He was never sure who chased whom, but he had never cared until now. He thought he had been caught, but looking back, he realized that Jessie had been his unwilling victim. He had pursued her, and she had never rejected him—much like this past weekend.

Once, when they were dating, he had tried to break the spell she had woven around him and asked another girl out to dinner. It had been the most boring night of his life! He hadn't been able to understand it. He couldn't even remember the girl's name anymore, although she had been beautiful, slim and intelligent. But her blue eyes hadn't sparkled with a secret wit, and her dark hair hadn't glistened like fire. He had been bored to tears and angry with himself for it. As they had left the restaurant, a small car had driven by. A redheaded laughing girl had glanced his way, and in a split second his eyes had locked with Jessie's. They had silently communicated eons of thoughts and feelings to each other, confirming what Philip had already known but would not admit. He loved Jessie. A bright red anger had blurred his vision as he realized that his best friend was in the driver's seat. Noah Weston was holding his woman's hand! He didn't know how he had taken his date home and dropped her off so quickly. But suddenly he was on Jessie's sorority-house steps, hands clenched at his sides as he waited for her return.

They were married two weeks later.

And he loved her more now than then. Somehow, with patience and time, perhaps he could win her back. *Perhaps* seemed like Mount Everest.

Wearily, he turned on the ignition and slowly drove the car away from Jessie's apartment.

5

The morning was hectic, as usual. The shopping-center workmen hadn't been able to get into the new store over the weekend to lay the floor. The manager of Jessie's store was out all day with the flu, and one of the other store managers was ill. Salesladies, confused by the new paper-work procedures, kept calling Jessie, asking for instructions and shipping information. By lunchtime, she was almost too tired to eat, but she knew that she had to sit and relax, away from the hubbub of the store. She went around the corner to a small luncheonette and propped her feet up on the chair across from her while she sipped a glass of iced tea.

The owner of Toodies Boutiques, Jay Peckman, was due to come by that afternoon. She had a hunch he was going to ask her to manage this store while he gave her present manager the new one. It wasn't exactly what she wanted, but she was pleased that he had already realized her worth at something more than selling.

She forced her body to relax, closing her eyes and letting her hands go limp.

Sleep had finally come in the early-morning hours, but when she awoke, that feeling of loneliness was still there. Her topsy-turvy emotions were still tightly entwined with Philip and the girls, but common sense told her she couldn't jump back into their lives as quickly as she had left, or the commotion that she caused would do more harm than good. She needed to be sure of what Philip and she wanted from a marriage before they could even begin to sort out their problems.

"Here you are. I've been to two restaurants, looking for you." Jay sat down across from her. He quickly noticed the tired circles under her eyes and the shoeless feet on the chair next to him. "You look bushed, Jessie. Is this job too much for you?"

She smiled. He was a dapper man who dressed a little louder and more flamboyantly than most men, but somehow it suited his personality. He was also consciously in love with himself and admiring of his prowess with the opposite sex. He was in his mid-forties, had recently been divorced and reveled in his new-found freedom. In fact, he thought of himself as a reincarnated Casanova.

"I'm fine. I had a hectic weekend, that's all."

The frown lines on his forehead disappeared. "Oh, that's all. I know how you feel. I've had a few of those myself." He chuckled.

"So I've heard through the grapevine," she said dryly but without malice.

His eyes widened. "And I didn't think you'd noticed."

"Noticed what?"

"That I'm sought after by every other good-looking woman. In fact, I'm considered entertaining and fascinating by most women—except you."

Jessie grinned, feeling better already. "That's not true. I just try to remember that you're my boss. Besides, you don't need me, with all the other women in your life just waiting for a chance to date you."

His brows rose. "Have you looked in the mirror lately? Not only are you smart, but you're damn good-looking. I'd have to be dead if I didn't enjoy having you across a dinner table from me while all the other older, more sophisticated men in the room drooled."

She laughed. "Where would we be dining? The geriatric ward?"

"See what I mean? Sharp mind. I like that. I also like your smile, even though I have to work hard for you to give me one."

"Perhaps that's why you like it. You have to work for it. Things are always valued more highly when they're not given away."

"So says a true Ben Franklin fan." His look was forlorn, designed to tug at her heartstrings. It didn't work. She laughed aloud, a deep throaty sound that seemed to come from the bottom of her toes. He smiled in return, his eyes not missing the fact that she was more tense than usual despite the laughter.

He ordered a salad for her, ignoring her protestation that she wasn't hungry, and a sandwich for himself, then sat back to discuss the previous week's business and that week's projected profits. They finally got around to the new store and its plans and problems.

". . . and I think the best man for the job is you. So what do you say? Would you like to manage the new store?"

She was stunned. She had never thought he would hand her a promotion over a club sandwich. Especially that promotion, which was exactly what she had wanted but hadn't been fool enough to hope for.

She finally found her voice. "Yes, yes, yes! And thank you."

"You're welcome." He smiled. "Besides, it's closer to your home, and you should know a lot about what the women in your neighborhood really want to wear. After all, you're one of the 'select' few who knows what a woman needs for the bridge club, PTA, a dance at the country club or a casual night at home with the neighbors."

A pain shot through the pit of her stomach, and she slowly placed her fork back on her salad plate before looking up at him with a steady gaze. "I think you should know that I used to be a member of that set, but I'm not anymore. I'm working for my living now. My husband and I are separated, and I live in an apartment not far from here. I just never changed my address in the records."

His brown eyes softened as if he understood the pain behind her thoughtfully chosen words. "I knew you were separated, Jessie; remember? But just because you're not a part of that life anymore doesn't mean that the experiences you had while leading it were for nothing." Sadness tinged his expression. "Everything that you do or have done has a bearing on what you are today. Good and bad."

She understood that he was speaking of more than just job qualifications. Jay Peckman hadn't wanted his divorce any more than Jessie had wanted her separation. It had just been something they had had to do in order to keep their sense of identity. He had known all along that she wasn't the type he should pursue, or he would have tried harder in the past months. Instead, he had recognized a hurting kindred spirit and had tried to tease her just enough to make her smile, but had never pressured her to oblige his whims.

She smiled again. "Suddenly, this salad tastes delicious!" she said, and earned his chuckle as a reward.

All that afternoon, Jessie worked at breakneck speed, the news of her promotion buoying her up, enabling her to get some of the back paper work done. But by the time she caught the bus to go home, her spirits were wilting again under the constant pressure she had forced herself to apply.

And when she reached home, her spirits deflated like a worn-out tire. Her quiet apartment rang with an emptiness that almost paralyzed her. For the past three months, she had worked hard to pull herself together and be a success in the business world, and that day she had achieved some measure of that success. But she couldn't seem to feel happy; instead, a deep, black depression fell over her shoulders like a hooded mantle. So what if she was the new manager of an up-and-coming dress shop? So what if she was slimmer and better-looking than she had ever been? So what if she had conquered her tattered emotions enough to glue them back together? There was no one with whom to share her accomplishments. Philip wasn't there for her to talk to, to share with, to laugh and make love with. Philip . . .

Suddenly, mentally and physically exhausted, she collapsed in a huddle on the couch and cried.

The phone rang a half hour later; Jessie had dried her eyes and taken aspirin for her headache, which wouldn't go away. She thought about letting it ring, realizing that it might be one of the salesgirls with a problem. The store was open late that night, and Tina, a relatively new employee, was temporarily in charge.

Wearily, she decided to answer it. "Hello?"

"Put your glad rags on and I'll be by to pick you up for the biggest steak in Texas." Jay's laughing voice echoed over the telephone.

"Oh? What's the occasion?" She chuckled.

"The boss owes his new manager a night on the town."

"Thanks, Jay, but I'm not feeling very well right now." That wasn't a lie. "But I'll take a rain check."

"If you don't have a fever, you'll do fine, Jessie,"

he ordered imperiously. Then his tone changed to one of quiet pleading. It was a tone that Jessie knew well. "Please, Jessie. No strings attached. I just want some uncomplicated company."

She sighed, giving in to his plea. "All right. Give me an hour." Why not? Was her apartment so thrilling that she couldn't bear to leave it for a little outside excitement?

"Forty-five minutes. Give me your address. All I have with me is the telephone number."

She was dressed and ready by the time Jay turned up, twenty minutes late.

"Let me get my jacket. I'll be right with you," she said over her shoulder as she walked into the bedroom.

As she entered the room, the telephone rang. Without thinking, Jay reached over and picked it up. His voice sounded loud and booming when he answered it, but as he held the phone toward her, he was more restrained. "I think I goofed. It's for you."

Jessie chuckled. "I imagine so, since this is my apartment."

"Jessie? Are you all right?" Philip's voice rasped down her spine, and she clutched the phone tighter. "Jessie?"

"I'm fine, Philip," she finally managed, her heart thudding down to her toes. "I was just leaving to have dinner with my boss." She could have kicked herself! Why was she explaining her actions to him as if she had to have his blessing?

"I see." There was a taut, stilted silence before

he continued. "I . . . uh . . . just thought you ought to know that Amy is ill. She's come down with the measles."

Her hand tensed, almost clutching the receiver. Ever since P.J.'s death she had reacted strongly to any kind of illness in the children. She had been told it was because she was afraid of losing someone again to death's dark visage. She didn't agree or disagree; she just knew that it frightened her terribly. She swallowed hard to keep the fear at bay. "Are you sure it's measles?"

"Mrs. Anderson seems to think so, and she's had five children. But I'll take her to the doctor in the morning and have him confirm it. I don't know how serious her case is, but if the amount of red spots have anything to do with it, she has it bad enough. You can't see a freckle on her nose."

"Is she feeling all right, or has she got a fever?" Jessie persisted, almost ordering him to answer her. But she should have known better.

Philip muttered an expletive under his breath. "Look, I'm sorry I called and interrupted your fun. You needn't worry. I'll take care of Amy. You go have a good time on the town tonight. I'll handle the children, just like I have ever since you left us."

The phone clicked, and the line went dead.

She quickly redialed, forgetting that Jay was standing by, waiting, watching. When Beth answered, Jessie gave a sigh of relief at not having to speak to Philip or Mrs. Anderson.

"Beth, this is Mommy, darling. Do you know if Amy has a fever?"

"Just a little one, Mother," her nine-year-old daughter answered politely. "We're playing cards right now."

Jessie's heart stopped its heavy thumping. After checking with Jay, she gave the name of the restaurant to Beth, making her write it down along with the phone number. She wanted to rush home and take care of Amy, but her common sense told her that everything was under control and that she would be better off not seeing Philip right then, considering the mood he was in. She talked to Amy for a few minutes, promising to come by after work the next day, then hung up. Her evening was ruined.

Nevertheless, she tried to keep smiling all through dinner, for Jay's sake as much as for her own. He was a delightful dinner companion, witty and easy to talk to, and before she knew it, she was pouring out her problems as if she had known him all her life.

"So that's why you're so dedicated to doing a good job." Jay's hand came out and covered hers, giving it a fatherly pat. Somehow she felt comforted by his action.

She smiled. "I love work. At first, I thought it was the answer to everything. Then I realized that, as much as I love what I'm doing, there's a part of me that misses—no, needs—my children."

"And your husband?" Jay's eyes softened as she visibly flinched from his words.

"That issue is dead. And so is this conversation." She flashed a small, determined smile at him before once more studying her plate.

"The issue may be dead, dear girl, but the marriage isn't." His dry tone was just what she needed to hear. "From all that's been said tonight, I think that he's a very lucky man. You just haven't told him so."

Jessie laughed then. She could just imagine herself standing on her tiptoes, nose to nose with Philip, and telling him how wonderful she was! "No, not yet," she said, but the light of battle was beginning to spark in her eyes. "But someday I will. As soon as I think he's ready to accept the fact."

Jay's eyes twinkled, and he gave her hand another squeeze. "Thatta girl!"

Jessie splurged on dessert, a fluffy, high-calorie concoction with almonds and slivers of semisweet chocolate embedded in rich whipped cream.

The ride home was quiet, with neither of them in the mood for conversation. The car radio spun out a sweet, rhythmic bossa nova tune. Jessie forced herself to sit up straight when they reached the driveway of her apartment. She turned in the seat, placing a hand on Jay's cheek.

"Thank you, friend, for my promotion and celebration. You're just what the doctor ordered."

He smiled in return. "So are you, Jessie."

The moment her key entered the lock, her thoughts were with Amy. Without taking off her jacket, Jessie went to the phone and dialed Philip. Suddenly, her panic was back. Was Amy really all right, or were they just telling her that? Reason told her that they weren't lying, but her brain couldn't seem to convince her heart of that fact.

"Hello, Mrs. Anderson? Is Philip there?" she asked when the telephone was finally answered.

"No, ma'am." The woman's voice was stiff and rigid with disapproval and just a touch of triumph. "Mr. Young left an hour ago. He took Amy to the emergency room."

Her heart ceased beating; her blood stopped flowing through her veins. Fear strangled the breath from her throat. She closed her eyes to shut out the vivid pictures of death. "Oh, my God!"

Philip tucked Amy into her bed, gave her the medication the emergency-room doctor had given him and quietly closed the door.

After a few whispered but reassuring words to Mrs. Anderson, Philip walked downstairs and headed directly for the crystal bottle that held his expensive twelve-year-old scotch. He uncapped it, and without ice or water to soften the liquor's potency, poured himself a glassful. He downed it as if he were drinking tea, quickly and with evident satisfaction. He poured himself another, then collapsed onto the couch cushions as if praying that they were the arms of Morpheus taking him away from everything he hated.

Amy was fine. She had the measles with a high fever that aspirin and a cool washcloth could have taken care of. He had panicked. And he had done so out of pure and simple guilt: After talking to Jessie and hearing that strange man's voice at the other end of the phone, he had gone just a little haywire inside. He had wanted to smash something, particularly the unknown man's face! He had wanted to hit out at someone, scream, anything! But he couldn't. He had to remain calm and in control in front of Beth and Mrs. Anderson. But for one brief flash of time, he had wondered how Jessie would react if she had found out Amy's illness was more serious than they thought—if perhaps she had been dying. Then Jessie would have to live with the guilt of knowing she had been playing around with another man while her child was dying. For one split second, his veins had run warm with vengeful satisfaction at the thought. Then he had realized what he was thinking, and reason had snapped back into place. He had felt deeply guilty at his thoughts. When he had gone up to check on Amy again, his guilt had made her fever seem higher, and he had panicked.

So he had spent the evening in the emergency room while Jessie was probably wrapped seductively in some other man's arms, listening to sweet, sexy words spilling into her ears and slowly melting with desire that until now only he had been able to ignite in her.

He gulped the rest of the drink down and put the empty glass on the coffee table with a thud.

That thought had haunted him all night long; he might as well face it now instead of hiding his fears away. No one was there to see him break down. He placed his head in his hands and shut his eyes to the intense pain.

His Jessie—and she had always been "his"— was probably in the arms of another man. His stomach muscles tightened as the thoughts he had violently rejected all night finally washed over him. "She's mine!" his mind screamed, but only the echo of her throaty laughter answered him. His fists clenched, and he struck out at the cushions on both sides of him.

For the first time since right after P.J. had died, Philip Young broke down and cried.

Jessie fumbled with the clasp of her purse as she pulled out money to pay the cab driver. She had called a taxi because she had been far too shaken to drive herself. Her steps after she left the cab were quick, almost running, as she reached the door of her home. Their home. Suddenly, her frenzied activity stopped. When she walked through the door and entered the house, she would know if Amy were all right or if she were so sick that she had had to stay in the hospital. Suddenly, finding out scared her more than not knowing.

She searched her mind for the combination to the door lock. They had had it installed over a year before, and it had taken the place of keys that could be lost or duplicated. Jessie had thought it a wonderful new invention at the time, but now it was delaying her entry to the house, and she hated it. She pushed the buttons, making an error in the sequence, then pushed the computerlike numbers again. Her hands were trembling and damp with perspiration. She held her breath as she waited to see if Philip had changed the lock. He hadn't. The door silently swung open, and she stepped inside.

The small lamp on the side table illuminated the hall. The house was deathly quiet. She stood in the center of the room, hearing a noise and finally placing it in the living room. Someone was crying. Her heart wrenched at the loneliness and utter despair of that sound. Jessie didn't know how she reached Philip's side; she didn't even realize she had almost run to him. She placed her hand on his shoulder and gave a gentle shake, all the while secretly knowing that she was too late.

"Philip? What happened? Please tell me, please!"

His head shot up in disbelief; then he buried his face in his hands again, furtively wiping the tears from his cheeks. "Nothing's happened. What the hell are you doing here?" His voice was a growl, a mean sound that sent a cold shiver down her spine. But his tears were real, and they more than anything else told her of the emotions that he was trying so hard to conceal.

"Is Amy all right? Is that it? Is she sicker than you thought? Please! Tell me! Please!" Her voice teetered on the edge of panic, and Philip realized why she was there. She wasn't a product of his wishful thinking; she was frightened—just as he had wanted her to be earlier.

She knelt down beside him, her hand skimming the side of his jaw as she searched his face for answers she didn't want to find. His eyes softened at the fear that was stamped on her lovely face. His hand covered hers, imprisoning it against the side of his face.

"She's fine. I panicked. I thought her fever had risen, and I decided to make sure she was all right." His voice was less cold and gruff, but it was still deep with emotions that were so close to the surface.

Closing her eyes tightly, Jessie took a deep breath. Relief flooded through her, finally allowing her cold, cramped muscles to relax. "Thank God," she murmured, bowing her head.

Her questioning eyes searched his, almost getting lost in their golden brown depths. "Then why are you crying?" Her voice became a soft whisper. "I've never seen you cry before. Never."

He let go of her hand and stood, pacing back and forth for a minute before making his way to the bar again. Jessie sank onto the plush carpet and used the couch as a brace for her back. She felt exhausted; her bones had finally turned to water. She watched him through ancient eyes. She felt as if she were a hundred years old.

Philip lifted the scotch bottle and raised an eyebrow in silent question, and she nodded slowly.

As he poured, he spoke. "I've cried before, Jessie. You just never knew it. It isn't acceptable for a man to be seen crying. Besides, I was always the one who had to be strong and dependable for you and the children."

"Of course," she replied bitterly. "Machoism is everything to a man."

"In a way, it is." He hesitated, picked up the drinks, then walked back to the couch. Reaching down to place the glass directly in front of her, he gave her a smile, then sat down. "Just like it's the woman who should keep the home fires burning, raise the children, care for her husband."

"But not all women can keep up that role. Some

of us just aren't capable of doing it without help."
She waved her hand in the air as if dismissing the
last word. "Oh, I don't mean housekeepers or
maids or cooks. I mean emotional support."

"I know what you mean." His voice was soft. He
reached out and tenderly touched the back of her
neck, as if his fingertips craved the feel of her skin.
"After I tucked Amy back in bed tonight, I came
down here and had a drink. I remembered a few
things that I had ignored before. It was hard
realizing that I hadn't been the man I thought I was.
It still is."

"What do you mean?"

"I remembered the time all three kids came
down with the flu and you had to handle them
alone. I had a business meeting that afternoon;
then I had dinner with a client. When I came home,
filled with elation over one of the biggest deals I had
ever put together, you were waiting. You were
exhausted, close to tears from being hassled by the
children, but you had ice in the bucket and a drink
waiting for me. You sat and listened to me for an
hour before you finally told me how rotten your
day had been." He took a gulp of his drink. "But
you had waited, and I had taken it for granted that
you would."

His touch was making the back of her neck tingle
deliciously. "And?" she prompted, trying to focus
on his words rather than his touch.

"And I gave you two or three platitudes that I
thought would serve the occasion. Later, when we
got ready for bed, I was in an amorous mood, and
you weren't. I remember I was irritated."

"So was I." She grinned at the memory. "But you soon talked me around to your way of thinking."

"Yes, because I wanted you. It didn't matter that you weren't in the mood. I wanted you. Then."

"I don't see where all this is going, Philip."

He sighed. "Nowhere. I just realized how selfish I had been." His hand dropped back to his leg. "Tonight, when you weren't here to tell me what to do with Amy, I was irritated, too. Then I realized that you had had to handle most things by yourself. If you *had* been here, I would have let you handle this by yourself, too. I cursed you for not being here until it finally dawned on me that you might have felt that way about me sometimes. I was scared."

"Did you hate me?"

"Hate you? No, I was angry. But the thought of you feeling that way toward me shook the hell out of my own self-confidence." His voice had a wry, mocking note.

"I know that feeling." She sipped her drink, her thoughts tumbling one over the other as she became aware that she hadn't bothered to notice the subtle changes in the man she had professed to love so long and so well.

"I thought you did." His voice was warm, sorrowful, as his hand came back to rest sensuously on the nape of her slim neck, awakening nerves that hummed in response. "Is it too late for us, Jessie? Is it really all over? Have I just been too stubborn to face it? Have I destroyed everything between us without knowing it? Are you in love with someone else? That guy who answered the phone tonight?"

For the first time since they had been married, Jessie realized her own strength. Philip was just as riddled with doubts as she had been. Yet, mixed with her new-found strength, there was a gentle, wondering tenderness. Why hadn't he spoken earlier of his feelings? Why hadn't she probed him before?

"One question at a time, please." She chuckled shakily. "First, I don't know if it's too late. I only know I had to run away from you. I was choking to death, and you had your fingers on my neck." His touch was instantly removed, and she chuckled again, reaching over her shoulder to find his hand and bring it back to her neck, holding it there with her own. Somehow it was easier to talk to him there, in that darkened room, when everyone else was asleep. She didn't have to face him, and that made it even easier. "You didn't destroy anything that I didn't have a hand in, too, Philip. Looking back, I think I could have fought harder for you, but I just didn't. I allowed myself to believe the worst even before it happened. No, I'm not in love with anyone. The man on the phone *was* my boss, and he was taking me out to celebrate my new promotion. That's all."

"I hate him," he said with unexpected vehemence.

"Don't bother," she said huskily, finally turning toward him, her eyes luminous in the dim light. "Put your efforts toward seducing me, Philip. I need you tonight. I need you more than I've ever needed you."

Her candor took his breath away. A gleam lit his

eyes as he devoured her with his look. His hand came up to stroke the side of her face, one finger following the curved line of her brow. Suddenly, he smiled. "Right now?"

She nodded. "Right now." His slow smile lit her heart.

"Even if I'm not in the mood?" he teased huskily, and she nodded again; this time her expression was solemn.

"Even if you're not in the mood," she repeated.

"Then come upstairs, Mrs. Young, and help me get into a better frame of mind."

"With pleasure, Mr. Young," she said softly, pulling him up from the couch so he could wrap his arms around her and hold her close to his heart. "With pleasure."

6

They climbed the stairs with their arms entwined, as if not touching would shatter the intimate moment they had miraculously created.

Jessie's heart beat like a fast-paced metronome, knocking against her rib cage in anticipation. She glanced up to see the brilliance in Philip's eyes, and it dazzled her, giving her a strength of will she had never known she possessed.

Ever since she and Philip had gotten married, she had wanted to be the aggressor, but she had held back, always too fearful of being rebuffed. That night would be her night.

Philip shut the bedroom door with his foot, swinging her gently into the enveloping cage of his arms at the same time. His mouth covered hers, homing in on her sweetness as if she were honey to be devoured, yet savored. His hands stretched across her back and pulled her closer to him until there was no room for even the clothing they wore. She could feel every bone and taut sinew in his body, leaving no room for doubt that his need for her was as great as hers for him.

"Wait," she murmured, pulling away. "You first. I've always wanted to undress you. Let me."

She unbuttoned his shirt, her hands straying every now and then to rub against the hair-roughened hardness of his chest. She pulled his shirt tail out and then slid the shirt off his shoulders, only to allow it to cuff his hands to his sides. Her fingers deftly undid his belt, then impatiently un-hooked the button of his pants and slid down the zipper. The noise sounded loud in the silent room, underlining the intimacy of the moment; then there was silence. Only Philip's breathing mingling with hers could be heard in the quiet. His pants and shorts dropped in a fluid motion, and she almost gasped at the magnificent structure of his tall, lean body. He was a gilded tan everywhere, resembling a golden, tiger-eyed cat more than a real, flesh-and-blood man.

Her eyes slowly cruised his body, warming to a brilliant blue as she watched his small nipples become as erect as her breasts felt full. Her tongue caressed a small bud, lavishing it with enough attention to pull a deep groan from the depths of his lungs. She turned her attention to the other one, not wanting to show partiality, and received the same response again. Her hands trailed across the breadth of his shoulders, down his arms and across his belly, and she felt him suck in air at her touch. It was a heady, powerful feeling to know that she was forcing him to respond to her that way when she was fully clothed and still in command.

She looked up at him through her lashes, only to be singed by the heat of his gaze. "Do you want me?" she asked throatily.

"You can see for yourself" was his equally throaty rejoinder. "Undo my cuff links so I can hold you, Jessie. Don't torture us both this way."

"In a minute," she promised against his partially opened lips. Her mouth brushed his; then her tongue flicked lightly against his parted mouth again, teasing and taunting him into waiting for her next move and his next pleasure. She tortured him as she had never done before. Her hands caressed his body everywhere but where he tried to direct her. Her lips nibbled on his flesh.

Her tongue outlined his mouth, making small, darting forays between his teeth before seeking another spot. She kissed the hollow of his throat and the shadowed curve of his shoulder, leaving warm, damp spots to cool in the night air and constantly remind him of where her kisses had been.

Her hands found the hard sides of his ribs just under his arms, and she lightly rubbed the area with her palms before letting them drift to his buttocks, kneading the flesh, then resting lightly on the side of his hips until she teased that part of him that needed her intimate contact most. She brushed by his need as she felt the more sensitive flesh of his inside thighs. She tilted her head up as her eyes focused on his, watching the play of lights that danced there and noticing the tautness of his jaw and shallowness of his breathing. He wanted to crush her in his arms, but his cuffs prevented that from happening, and his frustrations showed plainly on his handsome face. Reveling in the intense feeling of power she held over him, she felt the surge of twin emotions of loving and power that played through her system at his helplessness. Never before had she been so daring, so completely in control.

His shoulders rotated in rough, staccato movements, and she knew he was becoming taut with impatience. He had never been as helpless before. Always the aggressor, he wasn't able to stand being out of control for long.

"Don't you like being the object of my attentions?" she murmured seductively, the tip of her tongue teasing the whiteness of her teeth.

"I don't like it being a one-man show, Jess. Help me undo these damn cuffs." His actions continued, shoulders rotating, chaffing against the cloth of his shirt.

"Not yet," she murmured, loving his helplessness. "Soon, darling. Soon."

Suddenly, his arms were free and twining around her like strong vines. His touch was the brand of ownership, possessively claiming her soft skin as his own.

She was startled. "How . . . ?" she murmured.

"I had to touch you. Don't you see? I need you as much as you need me."

She buried her lips in the hair on his chest. "But you've prolonged *my* agony at times. It's not fair," she protested.

The remembrance of the times when he had done so passed across his face, and he grimaced at the painful memory. "I'm not as strong as you, Jessie. I need more."

She couldn't help the chuckle that rose in her throat at his admission. "Not more, Philip, just differently," she finally conceded.

His lips claimed hers in blatant possession, and without intending to, she melted against him. Her aggressive attitude toward him had lasted longer than she would have thought possible in the past, but she was happy to let him take the lead, showing her once more just how much he needed her.

Strong but impatient hands quickly unzipped her dress and silently tugged at the shoulder seams until it whispered away to a heap on the floor. His hands cradled her breasts, lifting and touching the fullness of them before finding the catch of her bra. With a trembling that gave evidence of his tight control, he released her from its imprisonment.

A deep sigh mingled in the air between them. "My God, you're sweet, Jessie," he murmured with velvety roughness against the creamy whiteness of her breast. "So sweet." As if to prove his point, he took her flesh into the warmth of his mouth.

Her breath caught in her throat, not allowing her to move or breathe in case the spell should be broken. A hypnotized, floating sensation swept over her, and she let herself flow with it. His magic touch was everywhere. The stirrings of need that had begun their lovemaking had turned into a stream of wanting that flowed through her veins like slow, warm pudding, sapping her strength and will totally. Jessie didn't know how she came to be on the bed; the night was a blur, and the only actions she was aware of were his. Philip's body and Philip's hands and Philip's mouth dominated her very being. His tongue traveled down her breasts, making a heated path as he touched all of her with his lips, pulling intense responses from her that she had had no idea she was capable of giving. It had always been good between them, but this feeling was created by a sorcerer, one who knew her well and played upon her soft, sensitive spots as if weaving an intricate, purposeful spell that had to be cast in just exactly that way.

She arched toward him, unable to wait for his possession any longer, and still he dallied with her.

"Now," she whispered, clutching his shoulders with fingers that dug into his flesh.

"Not like this. Like this," he answered before rolling on his back and pulling her to cover him with her flesh. They joined, and the joining became an ecstasy so great that Jessie thought she would die from the ever-spiraling intensity of it. She arched her spine, flinging her head back. His hands still cupped her breasts as if he were clinging to a life line. They moved in slow motion, neither ready to let their feelings dictate a faster pace. Slowly, slowly, she bent forward, her lips seeking his at the ultimate moment to blend more than just bodies, but spirits.

They came back to earth slowly. Philip's hands became lost in the damp curls of her hair, keeping her face next to his as if he were afraid that breaking their contact would shatter the experience they had just shared. Their breaths mingled as soft, quick gasps brought them back to sanity.

He kissed her cheek, her closed eyes, her chin, her throat. His hands trailed down to find the path of her spine and bring her closer to him. Slowly, their heartbeats slowed to a more even pace.

"I love you, Jessie," he muttered before heaving a sigh.

"I love you, too," she finally whispered to his sleeping body, tightening her clasp of him. "I just don't know if it's enough."

She was up early to make Amy's favorite breakfast: pancakes in the shape of zoo animals. Jessie kept a constant eye on the clock, knowing that she had to give herself forty-five minutes to dress and get to work. She would wear what she had worn the day before and pick up something new when she reached the shop.

Philip had still been asleep when she had crept from bed and into her daughter's room to check on her fever. Beth had already been up washing for school.

The door from the maid's room closed, and Jessie jumped, then turned to see the housekeeper's eagle eye on her. "Good morning, Mrs. Anderson."

105

"Morning," the older woman said stiffly. "What are you doing?"

"I'm fixing the children's breakfast. Beth is awake, and Amy will soon be up, too."

"That's my job."

Jessie flipped out the cooked pancakes and slowly lowered the spatula to the counter top, forcing herself not to slam it down. She stiffened, finally deciding that it was time to confront the housekeeper and make her place in the household known.

"I have run this household for years. I shall continue to do so for as long as I want to. Your job is what I decide it will be, and usually I would agree with you that breakfast is part of your domain. However, today I am cooking Amy's favorite breakfast. It's my choice." She shrugged. "But," she said, a thread of steel in her tone, "I refuse to be made to feel an outsider in my own home. Do I make myself understood?"

"Mr. Young hired me to cook and take care of his children. He didn't say anything about you coming back and disrupting things." The housekeeper kept her stiff stance, daring Jessie to say more. "I take my orders from Mr. Young."

"Very well. I'll give you a choice, Mrs. Anderson. You can stand by and become as frustrated as I will be by bucking me all the way, or we can work together and help both Mr. Young and the children. I will continue to work and can certainly use your help and cooperation." Her eyes sharpened. "But I can also live without it."

They stared at each other across the room, their strong wills charging the air with electricity.

Jessie held her breath, not daring to let the other woman know how intimidated she felt.

Finally, with rigid shoulders, Mrs. Anderson turned and went quickly back into her room.

Jessie's breath came out in a whoosh. Her hands were damp with perspiration, and her muscles felt cramped and stiff. Damn that woman for making her feel like the previous day's garbage! With jerky movements, Jessie turned back to the stove and begin pouring more batter in the pan, forcing herself to concentrate on the shapes she was making.

Arms came around her waist. "My bed got cold without you." Philip nuzzled her throat and the small crevices of her ear, sending sizzling messages down her spine and through to her toes.

Jessie's first instinct was to turn into his arms and let him take away the tension of the past twenty minutes by crying on his shoulder. Common sense reasserted itself, however, as she realized that she had always done that and then had regretted it later when things had been taken out of her hands. She had had a taste of being in control the night before. Indeed, she had been striving to achieve that control for the past three months. Was she willing to lose it now?

"Then it's a good thing I got up. You're late for the office, and pretty soon I'll be late for work."

She could feel his hands on her abdomen slacken. Flipping the pancakes out of the pan and onto a warmed plate, Jessie ignored his response. It was only seven-thirty in the morning, and already she felt as if the day should be over.

"What time do you have to be at work?" Philip moved away from her and poured himself a cup of coffee. She listened to the sounds she recognized so quickly: the cupboard opening, the cup being lifted out and placed on the counter, the sound of the coffee being poured. It was a ritual she had never known she missed until now.

"Nine-thirty."

"I'll drive you."

"No, I'll drive myself. We still have the station wagon, don't we?"

"Mrs. Anderson uses it."

Silence filled the room. Jessie readied a tray for Amy and a covered plate for Beth. Her actions were quick and decisive, not at all in keeping with the confused thoughts swirling through her mind.

Philip sat at the table, watching her every move. "Jessie?" he said softly, and she looked over at him, straight into his eyes, losing herself in their golden depths. "Will you be back tonight?"

He wasn't begging or pleading but asking directly; in doing so he was giving her the option of answering the same way. He was leaving the decision up to her.

For half the night, she had pondered the problem of staying or going back to her apartment alone. Half the night, when all the time she knew what she wanted the answer to be. She wanted to try to make the marriage work, but not at the expense of her pride. Would he accept that, even understand it, without her explaining it to him? She didn't know.

"Yes," she said simply, sitting down at the table and leaning toward him. "I'll stay for a while. At least until Amy's better," she said, giving an excuse they both saw through. A small, tender smile lit up her eyes from within.

He smiled in return, and her heart quickened its pace, suddenly making her feel young and foolish and happy. He was taking her without any soul-searching questions and answers. He, too, was willing to compromise. "Stay here for the Christmas holidays. They're less than two weeks away, and Amy will just be getting better."

She didn't have to weigh the decision. "Yes."

His hand covered hers, giving a light squeeze. "I'm glad."

Mrs. Anderson's door opened and closed. The older woman walked into the kitchen and took in the intimate scene in front of her. With a sniff, she turned and poured herself a cup of coffee, then pointedly stared out the window as she sipped loudly.

Philip and Jessie shared a conspiratorial grin, keeping the warm mood between them even though a dragon in the shape of a woman had entered their small enchanted world. Despite the fact that December's chill and bleak skies hung heavy outside, it was the beginning of a wonderful day.

* * *

The day sped by. Customers poured in, most of them last-minute shoppers seeking the perfect dress for a Christmas party. By the time five-thirty came, her feet ached, and her shoulder muscles were strained, but her smile was still intact. It had been a wonderful day!

She slipped on her coat and grabbed her purse, giving last-minute instructions to the part-time evening sales help. Philip was waiting.

The sleek gray Cadillac sat at the curb. Philip was behind the wheel and turned toward the passenger door with a smile on his well-chiseled mouth. His tawny blond hair was delightfully mussed from the cold wind outside. He looked terrific.

Jessie slipped into the seat beside him. "Hi," she said, her warm breath still blowing mist.

"Hi." His warmer lips covered hers in a quick, hard kiss that left her feeling tingly, as if she had just gulped a brandy and it was seeping through her bones and muscles, relaxing them with its fire.

"How did your day go?" she asked, trying, though unsuccessfully, to contain the sensual excitement of being near him. She didn't know what the change in her attitude was or where it had come from. She didn't even care. All she really knew was that she hadn't felt so strongly drawn to him since they had first married. Nor had she ever been as confident of his love, which shone from his eyes like a beacon on a foggy night. She could almost feel herself swelling, becoming more feminine, more womanly, under his gaze, and it both frightened and titillated her.

Philip grinned boyishly at her. "Lousy. I'm in the middle of preparing a brief, and my mind decided to take a vacation."

"Oh? What kind of vacation?"

"It keeps imagining me in a hotel with this sexy, skinny little redhead I know. We're trying out a waterbed and she loves it, but I keep getting seasick." His face looked solemn, as if he were trying to solve a puzzle, but his eyes twinkled with his teasing.

She tapped her fingertip against her lips. "I see. It sounds like a phobia to me. The only cure is to face it, head on, and see if reality is better than the dream."

His hand covered hers. "I was hoping you'd say that. I thought I'd make an appointment for both of us to try out your theory this coming Friday night."

"What about Amy?"

"Amy will do just fine with Mrs. Anderson. Besides, we can always return home after midnight, if that's what you want to do."

It was too intimate a moment for her to vent her fears about Mrs. Anderson and herself. But the thought of the morning's confrontation slowly wilted her smile.

"What's the matter? You don't like the idea?" He tried hard not to sound disappointed. For a flashing moment, Jessie remembered another time, early in their marriage, when Philip had asked her to get a baby sitter so they could have some time alone. Because it had been his idea, with his obvious needs behind it, Jessie had balked. Why did it always have to be when he needed her, yet nothing exciting happened when she needed him? Her conscience twinged at the unfairness of that accusation. It wasn't quite true. Whenever she had hoped and wished for him to come home, take her in his arms and romantically sweep her off her feet, she had been unable to relay that message to him. In fact, looking back, she realized that she had been afraid of giving him a clue as to her feelings. She had even stiffened her attitude toward him, as if she were paying for even *thinking* of doing some of the intimate things she had wanted to try. Fear of rejection had stood in her way all her life, especially with the one man she had loved so much. And still did, a small voice said.

"Jessie?" Philip's voice brought her back from her own mental meanderings.

"I'd love to try out my reality theory," she said in a husky voice, silently promising herself the unrestrained time of her life!

Philip drove by her apartment so Jessie could pack a few pieces of clothing and some incidentals. Neither was willing to admit aloud that she should be taking more clothing than she did. Although Jessie silently begged for Philip to order her to pack everything and move back in with him, she couldn't say the words that would let him know how she felt. Better for both of them to try their new living arrangement one day at a time than to have her move in, only to find that they were back where they had started.

Amy's fever was sporadic, her temperature dancing up and down all during the evening. By dinner time, her fever was up again, so Jessie fixed a tray and joined her daughter, sharing the meal with her in her room. They talked, laughed and joked through mealtime. Several times, tears threatened to spill from Jessie's eyes, but she held them back. She loved and missed her children so. Why was she doing this to them and Philip? And herself! She needed them, too! Not as an ego trip to show her worth to the world nor as a block to keep the real world at bay but because love was the most precious gift one could give or receive.

Before they had finished dinner, Jessie had decided to have a talk with Philip that night. It would be far better to get some things said between them than wonder what was on his mind. Was this just an interlude? Did he really want to try to piece their marriage back together, as she now did, but on terms that would suit both of them, or would he insist on having things all his way? She knew all the right questions to ask but had no idea what the answers would be, and that frightened her. But, with a determination that she hadn't known she possessed, she would carry this confrontation through to the finish.

The sound of low, sexy, saxophone music floated from the stereo and permeated the room with its sensual beat. In the corner, a lamp burned, dimly illuminating the whole room. Ice tinkled against Jessie's Waterford crystal as she watched through half-closed lids while Philip poured his own drink.

The children were in bed, Mrs. Anderson had retired for the night, and they were finally alone.

She studied him surreptitiously through her lashes. His blond mane, thick and slightly mussed, recreated the endearing little-boy quality that had first drawn her to him. But his tall, broad frame was totally male, and his smooth movements told of his vast experience in the social world. He glanced up and smiled slowly, as if a thought had crossed his mind that he was savoring, tasting with a connoisseur's palate. He walked toward her.

Jessie forced herself to relax on the couch. There was no reason for her to back off from him as if she were afraid. That reaction was just a residue of old habits, old ways of thinking. He had always had the ability to both please and frighten her, bringing out her inadequacies in the face of his perfection.

He sat down next to her, leaning toward her and allowing her to smell the scent of aftershave, soap and the wine on his breath. His leg touched hers, sending electricity to other parts of her body. His arm encircled her waist, and her confidence began to reassert itself. This time she wouldn't feel his silent condemnation of that extra roll of fat. There was none. Her figure was good, and she knew it. Her hair was still the rich golden-red color it had been when they married, her eyes still as periwinkle blue. She had good skin and teeth. For the first time ever, she felt as if she were an equal match for him, deserving of his attentions.

She stared into his eyes and saw that he thought so, too, and that pleased her, adding to her confidence. She glanced down at her glass, her long nail circling the rim. "Can we talk?" she asked huskily.

"By all means." He smiled, as if knowing that their talking would end up in bed and looking forward to it.

She looked back up at him, a slight questioning frown on her brow. "Do you think we can make a go of our marriage?"

"Yes." There was no hesitation in his answer.

"Why?"

"Because I love you and I think you love me. That's more than a lot of people can say after twelve years of marriage." His hand came up to her neck, one finger twining through a short, lively curl. "You're still my idea of heaven, Jessie. I can't turn that feeling off and on like a light switch. When you're gone, I want you with me. When you're here, I want the closeness we once shared and are still capable of having."

She hesitated, trying to put her feelings into words that he would understand. If Philip had his way, she was sure that the conversation would end right away and making love would be next on the agenda. But there were things that still had to be said.

"We both have to make adjustments and compromises."

His light brown eyes narrowed just slightly, and she could see his legal, argumentative mind at work. A smile tugged at the corners of her mouth. He was getting ready to defend his side of their relationship.

She decided to plunge in first. "I know I need to be more trusting from now on and not believe that every minute you're away from me you're with another woman . . ."

"I was never with 'another woman,' unless you're talking about female clients. There's been no one but you." Philip's eyes hardened at that old accusation. "I can't help what you think, Jess. I can only tell you the truth. I'd have too much to lose if I was caught in a lie now."

"Logically, I know you're right. But emotionally I never really believed I deserved you, and because of that, I've always secretly waited for someone to snatch you away from me. But you can help me conquer those feelings of distrust, Philip, just by giving a few words of explanation when you're busy in the evening with clients."

"I don't understand."

"I need to know their names and why you're taking them out. It would put my mind at rest."

He thought it over and slowly nodded. "That's fair." He smiled. "Sometimes I forget to explain, but it's not because I have any secrets. I just get too busy. What else?"

"I want—no, I need—to continue working. I've been offered a promotion, being manager of the new Toodies. I want to be able to accept the challenge."

"Fine." His hand once more began rubbing the back of her neck, his thumb soothing the sensitive area just under her ear. His mind was obviously straying from the conversation to other areas of their relationship.

"That may mean working late three or four times a week until the store is running smoothly."

"Is that really necessary?" Now his brow furrowed.

"Is it necessary for you to take your secretary out to dinner once a month?" she asked quietly, without the usual accusatory tone she normally used.

But he took offense, anyway. "If we're both working late and I've kept her from dinner, I think it's only reasonable. Would you rather I told her to take thirty dollars and eat by herself?"

She wanted to scream *Yes!* but knew she couldn't.

Philip gave a heavy sigh, running one hand through his blond hair. "I didn't mean to fly off the handle. In the course of business, I often have to entertain outside the office. If the people I have to entertain are women, am I supposed to say, 'I'm sorry, but my wife won't let me eat with another woman unless she's here to make sure I don't have an affair under the restaurant table?'"

Jessie chuckled. The thought was ludicrous.

Philip joined in her laughter. He smoothed back the riot of curls that framed her eyes. "Darling, I love you. Only you. Please trust me." His lips hovered over hers, tantalizing, tempting, promising all sorts of wondrous feelings when he finally touched her. "Please," he whispered before ending her torment and claiming her for his own. Her heart sang with feelings she had thought were lost. But they were back, stronger than ever. All the love she felt for him was poured into her kiss, and his low groan told her that he understood her deep love and would always be grateful to her for it. Their passions continued to spiral until they were both naked and resting in each other's arms, feeding their love with a fire that couldn't be dampened except by a quenching touch.

7

Mrs. Anderson had declared a silent truce. Jessie had no idea how long it would last, but she was thankful that it existed at all.

The first three days after her return home were filled with activity. She always managed to have breakfast with Amy before going to work. Then she'd rush through dressing and catch a lift with Philip, who had so far managed to wait patiently for her. After work, Philip picked her up, and they would shop for Christmas presents for the children. It was the first time that Philip had helped with that chore, and it made the job much more fun. His sense of humor and wry comments put it on the level of a date, adding to the sensation of togetherness that was being reinforced daily. By the time evening came, she'd be exhausted from the never-ending round of chores, but she would catch her second wind after they had eaten dinner. Beth had become a little more vocal, though she was still not as spontaneous as she had been. Still, progress was being made. After dinner, Jessie would help Beth with her homework and then read a story to the girls. Amy, in particular, flourished under her mother's attention. Their delight at having their mother back gave Jessie added energy instead of tiring her out. She finally had what she wanted: the best of both worlds.

And after the girls went to sleep, her time with Philip was even more precious. She told him of her work and what it meant to her, the changes she was making, the decisions she had helped to make. And he listened. When he told her what had happened that day at his office, she understood the underlying circumstances and could relate better to his job because of her own new sense of worth and growing knowledge of the business world. It showed, making them more aware of each other as individuals.

But the times she loved best took place in the middle of the night. Then she would turn over and find Philip reaching out for her. He would curl her into the contours of his lean body, heaving a sigh of contentment that she was there, with him, as if she made everything right and real and wonderful. Those nights were stored away in the treasure house of her mind to be brought out and remembered in the middle of the day when she was at work. No matter what problems arose, she knew he would be there at night. Even though she loved her work and the sense of self-worth it gave her, she found that Philip and the girls meant far more.

It thrilled her to know that they needed her, too, but it was also a terribly frightening responsibility. What would happen if she and Philip couldn't make it together? She tried hard not to think of that possibility, but knowing that it was a trial period for both of them made it difficult.

When Jay Peckman called to tell her that they needed to meet after work at the new store to go over the plans for the racks and back-room storage, Jessie was disappointed. She had wanted to spend a quiet evening with Philip. But the store was nearing its opening date and had to be finished before the new salesladies could be interviewed and the stock unpacked. Time was running out.

She called Philip's office, but his secretary smugly informed her of his absence. He was in a meeting on the other side of town. Would she care to leave a message? No, she wouldn't, thank you, and Jessie hung up, unreasonably angry with herself for reverting back to her earlier animosity toward the woman.

She quickly called home and gave the message to Mrs. Anderson, who stoically promised to pass the news to Philip that Mrs. Young would be working late and would return home by eleven.

When she arrived at the new store, the workmen were still sawing and hammering as they partitioned the back room into sections, one for dressing rooms, one for receiving merchandise, and one for her small but adequate office. Jay stood in the center of the room, blueprints laid out on a drawing table as he scanned the walls, then checked them against the plans.

"Have you solved the mystery of the Pyramids yet?" Jessie teased.

His smile was spontaneous. "No, but I have discovered a big error. You have two more feet of back-room space than you should." His glance flicked back to the workmen, and his smile vanished, replaced by irritation. "Damn them! They should have measured, not eyeballed it!"

"What's the big deal? Two feet isn't a crime, is it?"

"It will be when the racks we had special ordered are too large to fit the remaining wall space."

"Oh," Jessie said softly, finally understanding his dilemma. Apparently, there was more to the building business than she realized. Who would have thought it mattered? She glanced over his shoulder at the blueprints and shook her head. She was able to locate the front door and the back room, but everything else was a mystery.

Jay grabbed the plans and walked to the back, stepping over electrical cords and piles of lumber on his way to talk to one of the workmen. Jessie watched them as they argued back and forth, each shaking his head or motioning toward the walls, but she could hardly hear a word because the electric saw was so loud. The contrast between her boss and the workman was so funny that Jessie began to shake with laughter. Jay was wearing navy blue pants with a blue and white checked sport coat. His shirt was so white it looked blue, his hair combed so that not a wave was out of place. His speech was filled with two-dollar words, some of which even Jessie hadn't heard.

The workman was a large man, overpowering Jay in both height and width. His baseball cap covered only the top of his long hair. His face was lined, and his cigar looked as if it were glued to the side of his mouth. Every other idea was emphasized with a swear word as he angrily explained, in loud tones, the placement of the wall and what he thought of it. Yet they both stood there and shouted at one another as if they spoke the same language!

It took Jay almost an hour to get the workmen to understand how imperative it was to have the wall moved back. Then, by the time he and Jessie had gone over the floor plan of the racks, dressing rooms, cashier's desk and displays, it was after ten.

"Buy you a drink? They have a bar here in the mall that serves all those fluffy drinks women seem to like so well," Jay said, a twinkle in his eye.

"Thanks, but no thanks. I'm tired and going home. I haven't checked on Amy this evening, and I want to make sure she's all right."

The twinkle left. "Do you call her by phone or run by the house?" he asked in a deceptively casual tone.

Jessie could feel herself blush. When she had talked to Jay over the phone this past week, she had deliberately refrained from telling him she had moved back with her family. She didn't know why she hadn't said anything any more than she knew why she felt as if she had been caught in the act of committing a crime now.

"I . . ." she began, only to see by his expression that he already knew.

"I had a feeling you had moved back in with your husband," he said, "especially when I couldn't get ahold of you by phone night after night."

Her brows rose in surprise. "You tried to call me? Why?"

"Because I was concerned about you. I knew that the night I took you to dinner you weren't really there, but mentally at home with your daughter."

She reached out and touched his arm, giving a light squeeze. Dear Jay! "I'm afraid I wasn't able to rest until I saw her, so I went home."

"And stayed there?"

"And stayed there. For now."

"Have you told your husband how terrific you are yet?"

She chuckled, remembering their conversation. "Not yet, but I'm warming up to it."

"Good. You're a pretty wonderful lady, Jessie. He had better appreciate you," Jay growled, hiding his feelings beneath his gruffness. But he didn't deceive Jessie. He really did care. Somehow that felt like a heavier burden than it should have.

As Jessie left the shopping center and headed toward the small taxi stand, she mentally shrugged her feelings of guilt away.

Jay was her boss, and Phil was her husband, and the two should never be confused. Somehow her instincts told her that they should never meet, either. It was then that she remembered the Toodies' open-house party scheduled for that Friday. A shiver ran down her spine, and she gathered her coat closer to her throat.

Philip was sitting in the living room, sipping a drink, when Jessie got home. His look was bland, his lean body casually draped against the couch. But his eyes told a different story.

"How did your business meeting go?" Did his voice hold just a hint of anger?

"Fine. The workmen put the wall in the wrong place, and the racks haven't come in yet, but we still have some time." She plopped down next to him and rested her head on the back of the sofa. Suddenly, she was exhausted. "Have you seen Amy? Is she all right?"

"Amy's fine." Philip downed the rest of his drink and stood, staring down at her. "Is that job too hard on you? You look tired."

"I enjoy my work, but I am tired," she said, her eyes still closed.

"If it tires you out like this, it can't be good for you."

"Why? Doesn't your job sometimes tire you out?"

"It's not the same. I have to work to support us. You don't. I don't like seeing you exhausted like this."

"Philip, please. Don't hound me. I enjoy my work, whether you think it's necessary or not. Besides, you could probably retire tomorrow and

we'd have enough money to live on comfortably."
Her voice had hardened, and her eyes had opened
to stare into the golden-brown depths of his. He
looked so vulnerable!

He strode to the bar, where he slammed his glass
down on the polished wood surface. "Good
night."

Jessie turned around, resting her arms on the
back of the couch. "Philip?" He stopped and
looked hard at her, and she took a deep breath,
continuing before she lost her nerve. "There's an
open house for the new Toodies this Friday night.
Will you come with me?"

"I thought we were going to have a private
celebration of our own." His voice was stiff with
anger.

She suddenly remembered their playful conversation about trying out waterbeds in a hotel. "I
know, but we can go to the party first, can't we?"

Silence echoed between them as they stared at
each other. Jessie wondered what had happened to
make his attitude change so much from what it had
been earlier. Could he be angry because she had
had to work late? But why? Hadn't he done so on
numerous occasions in the past, sometimes without
even bothering to let her know in time to change
plans that had been made? Her anger suddenly
came to the fore.

"Never mind. If you have to think about whether
or not to join me, then I don't want you to come."

"I'll be there," he said before walking out of the
room and up the darkened stairs.

Jessie listened to his footsteps echo through the

house, and her heart took another dive. Somehow everything had gone wrong in the space of a single day.

But when she went upstairs later, he was in bed, waiting for her.

His arms curled around her slight body and brought it into intimate contact with his own. One hand possessively cupped her breast, his thumb flicking over the nipple before settling down for the night. His legs fit intimately between hers, rubbing seductively against her flesh to awaken her to his presence. As if she could forget! His chest hair scratched delightfully against her back, bringing to life nerve ends she had never known she had. She snuggled close to him and gave a sigh. This was where she wanted to be, and apparently he felt the same way. But there was always a small hidden fear that seemed to pop into her head in the dark of night. Every time she felt safe and happy in Philip's arms, something happened. Would she ever really be happy again? Or would she and Philip tear each other apart until there was nothing left? She didn't know.

Jessie worked hard. Philip still took her to work, but she usually came home in a cab because of late-evening meetings with Jay. Discussions of stock differences and office furniture or interviewing women for the new store kept them both late.

Philip was polite but cool, only allowing her to get close to him in bed, when he pulled her into his arms to hold her next to the curve of his own body. At those times, she felt like a talisman that kept away the bad dreams. But most of the time she felt as if she were invisible. Amy and Beth saw her, talked to her, laughed with her, but Mrs. Anderson and Philip practically ignored her. A year earlier, she would have been devastated by his actions and intimidated by Mrs. Anderson. But not now! Now she was angry!

She had notified the caterers, informed the mall office that they would be open late and told the staff of each store the time and location of the open house. All she had to do was show up. She hoped.

The manager of her old store was slightly miffed that the new store had been offered to Jessie, but she wasn't as surprised as Jessie had thought she would be. Apparently, everyone but Jessie had known what a wonderful job she was doing.

Philip picked her up from work, and they drove home in silence. Jessie wished it could be one of those companionable quiet times, but her tight nerves told her that he was as tense as she was. After dinner, she read a story to Beth and Amy, who was enjoying her illness to the hilt.

"Mommy, you'll be right back after the party, won't you?" the little girl asked in an almost-perfect imitation of a breathless and very ill child. If Jessie hadn't seen her hopping up and down on the bed just a half hour earlier, she might have been concerned. As it was, she forced herself to ignore the fears that lay just beneath the surface and pretended to chuckle.

"I'll be here when you wake up, you little minx," she said, tickling Amy's ribs and enjoying her laughter. "So stop acting sick and turn over and go to sleep." She gave Amy and Beth a quick kiss, stooping to smooth the older girl's hair away from her big golden-brown eyes. They were just like P.J.'s had been. For a minute, her heart ached for the loss of her son, but only for a moment. Wasn't she lucky to have two such wonderful, bright children? she asked herself. Some people had no one, and she had so very much. If only Phil . . .

She stood. "Good night, girls. See you in the morning," she whispered before turning out the light and walking out the door.

"Mother?" Amy's reedy voice floated to her. "You won't shut the door all the way, will you?"

"No, darling. And I'll leave the hall light on," she promised. She had finally gotten Amy to turn out the light in the room as long as she left the door cracked. Progress.

Philip waited for her at the bottom of the stairs. When she reached his side, he smiled and held out his hand. "Pax?" he said in a husky voice, offering her the kiss of peace.

She couldn't help smiling in return, then placed her hand in his. Once again, electricity shot between them. Her eyes widened as she stared at him, melting into the golden depths of his intense stare. They stood that way for a moment, as if time itself had stopped, allowing them to catch up with it.

"Pax," she breathed in barely a whisper.

He opened his mouth to say more, but no words came forth. Instead, he tilted his head toward her, his eyes holding her a willing captive as she waited for his touch. His blond hair caught the light from the chandelier, which turned it to molten gold as he leaned down and softly, slowly, covered her lips with his for one brief, ecstatic moment. Jessie held her breath, automatically reaching for the side of his jaw, feeling the smoothness of his just-shaved skin and filling her nostrils with the scent of his after-shave. Her stomach clenched in reaction, her legs turning limp, like a wilted flower stem. The power of his kiss was so potent that it threw everything else out of her head. She didn't want the kiss to end. She wanted him to explore her more deeply, to take her in his arms and not let her go. Instead, his lips left hers, and he took a step back, a small smile of satisfaction on his face.

"Ready?"

She nodded, taking a deep breath to bring herself back to the present. His control angered her until she glanced surreptitiously through her lashes and realized that although he was acting as if nothing had happened, his chest was moving as rapidly as hers as he tried to catch his breath. A small smile teased her lips. Mr. Young wasn't as invincible as he seemed. Why hadn't she noticed that before? Her blue eyes twinkled at the obvious answer. Because she had always been too busy noticing her own responses to pay attention to his.

Champagne bottles were popping, hors d'oeuvres were being snapped up, and the crowd buzzed like a disturbed bee's nest. Jessie and Philip stood at the entrance of the store. Jessie noticed with pride all that had been accomplished in the past week, while Philip seemed to notice what hadn't yet been completed.

"This is going to open Monday?"

"You should have seen it last week. Now at least we have the walls and woodwork painted, the counter complete and the carpet on the floor." She glanced down and scuffed her toe, checking to see if the pale candlelight-colored carpet was as plush as it was supposed to be. It was. "We're ready to start accepting the stock from the other stores on Monday. They've received our first shipments for us and have tagged and steamed the dresses so that everything will be ready at the same time."

There was no more time to stand and talk, because Jessie, the woman of the hour, had been spotted. Several of the women engaged her in conversation, taking her away from Philip's side.

Philip strolled over to the champagne table and poured himself a drink. For the first time in his life, he felt out of place. He chug-a-lugged his drink and poured another, glancing around occasionally to see Jessie deep in conversation with someone else.

"A regular powerhouse, isn't she?" A flamboyantly dressed, slightly older man stood at Philip's side. He, too, was watching Jessie. Finally, he turned and held out his hand. "I'm Jay Peckman, owner of Toodies and Jessie's boss."

Philip's hand stiffened at the announcement, even though he followed through with the handshake. "I'm Philip Young."

Jay topped his glass off with the half-empty bottle of champagne sitting next to Philip. "Yes, I guessed as much."

"And you're the man who takes her to dinner and spends the evenings here 'going over plans' for the store." Philip sneered, a seething anger apparent in his voice, if not in his face.

"Correct again, counselor."

Philip stared at Jessie, who was animatedly talking to one of the other women, a manager, if her purple-ribboned name tag was correct. The weight Jessie had lost had been just enough to emphasize her slim waist, full breasts and enticingly curved hips without making her seem too thin, as he had once suggested to her. Her dress, a deep royal blue, hugged her petite figure, and the color set her hair on fire. She looked as if she were twenty-five years old. Her face was alive with expression; her eyes sparkled; her hands moved gracefully in conversation. If he hadn't known her and had been seeing her for the first time, he would have been drawn to her all over again. She was lovely! His hand knotted at his side. His loins ached; his mouth watered. He wanted her so badly that he had to hold himself back so he wouldn't barge into the crowd of women, fling her over his shoulder and walk out. She was his, damn it! Why was it that he knew it and she didn't?

Jay glanced at Jessie, then back to her husband. "She's a woman to be proud of, Young."

Philip's eyes searched the other man's. Was he trying to tell him something? If he was, why was he beating around the bush? "Say what's on your mind, Peckman."

"I just did." Jay's voice was filled with disgust.

He turned and walked toward a small group in the corner, instantly becoming one of them as he discussed the latest method of inventory control.

Philip cursed himself under his breath. What the hell was the matter with him? In the twelve years of their marriage, he had never been jealous of Jessie. Not really. Oh, possessive, perhaps, but he had always known she adored him, that she would put up with him and his small failures in the finer points of romancing her. Suddenly, he wasn't sure of anything. He was out of his element and didn't know how to make himself a part of such a gathering, a part of Jessie's new life. And he desperately wanted to belong with her. He gulped down his second drink and poured another.

A thought hit him, and he stared once more at Jessie.

Was the way he was feeling now something that she had felt at all those cocktail parties he had dragged her to? Had she experienced the same sensation of being out of place while the men stood around, smugly talking law over their wives' heads, as if women were just slightly brighter than children? Because that was the way he felt now. The women seemed to know their business inside out: inventory, seasons, displays, designer labels. They were speaking another language as far as he was concerned. They certainly didn't sound like what he had expected. But then, what *had* he been expecting? Something along the lines of recipes, children, in-laws? He was a fool!

One of the men in another group walked over to

refill his glass, a satisfied smile on his mouth as he grinned at Philip conspiratorially.

"Some girls, huh?" He nodded his head toward the group of women standing with Jessie. "Tank Wright here." He held out his large hand, carefully holding his champagne glass in the other. He looked as out of place in a dress shop as Philip felt. He was a huge man with a massive stomach to match. His clothing was well tailored but couldn't hide the fact that a tent would have done better at concealing his girth. "I belong to that little pasta maker over there," he said proudly, pointing to a woman who was part of a small group heading into what would be the office. "She manages the Toodies in Plano."

"Philip Young." Philip stuck out his hand, which was enveloped in the bigger man's, then almost crushed in his grip. "My wife is going to manage this store."

"Oh, I know all the company business," the bigger man wheezed before sipping from his dainty glass. "That's some coup. But I hear she's dy-no-mite!"

"Really?" Philip raised one eyebrow, tilting his golden-blond head. What the hell was this man talking about?

The larger man's eyes grew round as saucers. "Didn't your little lady tell you that everyone from salesclerk up was vying for this store? Even her manager thought *she* had it in the bag."

"But Jay Peckman thought better." Philip ground his teeth in frustration as he sought out the man who had put his wife in charge. Damn him!

Didn't he realize that Jessie only *looked* competent? She needed help in standing on her own two feet!

"Jay and several others. Your wife was the one the other stores called when things got rough or out of hand. You've got quite an executive there. My wife has wished on more than one occasion that she had the quick mind your wife does. But I guess you already know that." Tank guzzled what was left of his drink, then poured himself another before turning back to shake hands once more.

"Been a pleasure meetin' you. I'm sure we'll run into each other again at one of these shindigs. Take care, ya' hear?" The large man sauntered across the room to envelop his petite wife in a one-armed hug.

By the time the party was winding down, Philip was more confused than ever. Was his wife the same woman who had suffered a breakdown almost two years before, or was she this high-powered executive who handled things so capably? He had finally joined her and listened to the way she discussed the business so smoothly. The only conclusion he could reach was that she was a female Dr. Jekyll and Mr. Hyde. But there was another emotion that flowed through to his very bones that he was slower to recognize. He was jealous.

Jessie had created a career, a niche for herself, in just a few short months, and the results were staggering. She was confident, competent and damn sexy! And he had had nothing to do with her transformation. In fact, it hadn't taken place until she had left him. It hurt, and that, added to his other confused emotions, was making him reel with the enormity of it. The topper was that he didn't want to think of that now; he just wanted to get her out of there and into his arms. He ached to hold her next to him and feel the silkiness of her skin against his own. But more than that, he wanted to know that she was his. Totally and completely.

Someone said something to him, and he smiled grimly, nodding his head. He didn't know what the woman had said, but his nonanswer seemed to satisfy her. His eyes returned to Jessie, watching her sparkle as she said good-by to a departing couple, and he heaved a silent sigh of relief. Perhaps they could get out of there soon.

He downed another glass of champagne and slowly worked his way over to the table to pour himself some more. It was easier to stand in front of the table and drink than it was to stand next to Jessie and not sip from her lips. Damn!

It took another hour for the rest of the employees to leave and the clean-up crew to do their job. By that time, Philip had had several more glasses of champagne. Still, the ache for Jessie's body wouldn't go away.

But soon, soon, he'd have her with him, in bed, and then he'd be able to capture her attention all for himself. A look of satisfaction flashed across his face. At that precise time, Jessie glanced up. Her expression turned quizzical as she watched him down another glass. What was on his mind? She shrugged off the thought as she turned and gave an order to one of the crew. She'd find out his thoughts in just a few minutes, she was sure. Philip was never one to hold in his anger or his love. She just didn't know what mood he was in.

The skin on the back of her neck prickled, telling her that he was once more staring at her. He'd been doing that all night. Was her slip showing? Had her makeup worn off? What was the matter with him?

8

~~~~~~~~~~~~~~

With the exception of Philip's odd behavior, the evening had gone pretty well. Jessie felt satisfied with it. She had made friends with a few of the managers she hadn't met before and had reinforced working relationships with others. All the stores had to work harmoniously together in order for the chain to perform well. She leaned back in the plush interior of the car, finally relaxing her tense shoulder muscles. Yes, overall she was happy with the way the evening had gone. Except for Philip.

"Are you sure you're capable of driving?"

"Why wouldn't I be?"

"Because you drank *mucho* champagne."

"I didn't know you noticed."

Her brows arched in surprise. "Why wouldn't I? You'd notice if I did something like that."

"Only because I would be trying to protect you from making a fool of yourself."

"Oh, and you'd never make a fool of *yourself*, would you?" Her voice held a wry note.

"Yes, and I probably have, but you never noticed before." Before she could express the anger his words had fueled, he took her hand and placed it on his thigh, covering it with his own. "Please, Jessie, let's not argue tonight." His voice was low and seductive. "I missed you."

Once more, her brows rose in surprise. "But you were right there!"

"But *you* weren't. You were busy with everyone else."

"You could have mingled more," she retorted. "After all, you're not a child who has to be led by the hand into a social situation."

He nodded. "Yes, but I felt out of place. You seemed to know everyone, and the conversation revolved around your business." Jessie could see him smile ruefully in the dim interior of the car. "Would you believe that an attorney doesn't really get into stock reduction and ordering or inventory depletion? Your business associates really seem to know their business. And I don't."

"Ahhh," she said, reading between the lines and becoming tickled by his transparency. "So it was boring for you, and all you wanted was for the party to end so you could feel safer, more comfortable ground beneath your social feet."

She squeezed his thigh. "That's all right, honey. You did fine. Everyone liked you." A giggle threatened to escape, but she held it in—barely. How many times had these circumstances been turned around? She couldn't count them! But she did remember the times when she had confided to him that she had felt awkward in similar situations, and now he had said almost the same thing!

Philip must have remembered, too, because a chuckle finally escaped him. "You're a vindictive witch," he murmured, tilting his head so he could kiss the softness of her cheek. His lips branded her with his touch, and she almost backed away from the electricity of it.

"I wish I *were* a witch. Then I'd twitch my nose, and we'd be on a tropical isle, the wind blowing gently over the sand. Or we'd be on a waterbed, curled up in each other's arms and wondering what the poor people were doing."

"Probably the same thing, sans the waterbed or the island."

"Philip, let's go to that hotel now." She nibbled on his ear, her hand straying up his thigh. Her breasts curved to fit the contours of his side, pressing gently but firmly to remind him of her femininity.

But he apparently needed no reminder, because his hand sought and found the gentle slope of her neck as she leaned her head to rest on his shoulder. He took a deep, wistful sigh. "I'd love to, but because of this party, I thought we ought to delay it, so I gave Mrs. Anderson the day off tomorrow. She wants to leave early in the morning to visit her sister."

"Mmmmm, good," Jessie murmured, nuzzling his neck and distracting his attention once again.

"That means I don't have to share the children tomorrow. They're all mine."

"They always were, Jessie. You know that."

"Yes, but tell your housekeeper that and see the reaction you get."

"Are you having trouble with Mrs. Anderson?" His voice showed the depth of his concern, and suddenly she pictured him confronting the woman, or her, with their aversion to each other. No, this should be their own private war, not Philip's.

"No, I just sometimes think she's too possessive of the children."

She could feel him relax once more. "She cares for them a great deal. I was lucky to find her." It was said without malice, but Jessie felt the recrimination despite his bland tone.

The mood was shattered, and her spirits plummeted.

Her happiness didn't return. When they pulled into the garage and entered the house, they were silent, wrapped up in their own thoughts.

"Would you care for a nightcap?" Philip loosened his tie as he approached the bar.

"No, thanks. I'm tired. I think I'll check on the children and go to bed."

Her feet dragged up the stairs. After checking the children and kissing them both, she went to their bedroom. Should she sleep in the guest room? No. Philip had said nothing but the truth, and that wasn't a reason to be angry. That she was angry with herself for not being able to cope several months before was no reason to punish either of them now.

Her dress and slip were cast aside, her lacy bra unsnapped. She slipped under the coolness of the covers, turning her back to the door and curling her legs up. She forced away the thoughts of guilt that still seemed to riddle her. Deep, uninterrupted sleep was what she needed most.

Philip downed his brandy in one big gulp as if it were life-giving air.

Why in the hell was he down there, in the living room, when what he wanted most was upstairs in his bed? He rethought the evening, and a heaviness he couldn't explain filled his very being. He suddenly realized why he was so depressed and anxious, and the realization was like a blow to the gut, knocking his breath away. Jessie didn't need him to survive. She was very capable of surviving on her own. It was a hard fact to accept after twelve years of believing he was her very reason for existence. How egotistical could he have been!

His footsteps echoed in the hallway as he followed Jessie's earlier path. So why was she there? Because of the children? It must be; she certainly didn't need anything from him except what they were best at together: sex. In all the years they had been together, it was the one thing that had grown astoundingly better with time.

Straightening his shoulders, he faced the closed bedroom door. He felt as if he were a condemned man about to commit another crime. Well, if it were true that all they had to share was sex, then he'd better make the most of it and build from there.

He walked quietly into the room and stood at the foot of the bed, staring at the shadows the sheet made as it covered and clung to Jessie's slim body.

Jessie was becoming his entire world as no one had ever been before. Yet something in him shouted aloud the fear that he was losing her. She was slipping away from his grasp, and he didn't know how to hold on to her. As elusive and many faceted as the most brilliant of rainbows, his need for Jessie was more complete and all encompassing than he could admit even to himself.

His suit followed the same path as Jessie's clothing had. He crawled into bed; then he touched her shoulder, gently turning her around to face him. Still asleep, she nestled her head on his arm, and he could feel the silkiness of her skin, touch her nearness, smell the delicious fragrance of her hair. A lump in his throat choked off his breath. One small silvered tear dropped from his eye to dampen the pillow below.

Whether she was there or in her own apartment or across the world, Jessie was in his soul. He loved her more now than he had ever thought possible.

Closing his eyes, Philip sighed and fell asleep, his warm hand unconsciously seeking the softness of her breast, as if finding the perfect spot to rest upon.

Jessie felt the warmth of his body next to hers. She opened her eyes and looked up at his face. In sleep, he was relaxed, contented. Yet there was a pinched look around his eyes that told her that something was troubling him. Her hand was resting on his firmly muscled abdomen, and she carefully reached up and touched the golden hair on his brow.

She loved him with all her heart.

Why had it taken her mind so long to see what her body had known all along? He was everything that she needed and more. Oh, work was important. Hadn't it given her the time and perspective to view herself in another light and to be proud of the accomplishments that highlighted her own worth? Hadn't it given her the opportunity to get to know herself and grow stronger for the knowing? But work wasn't enough. More than anything else, she needed Philip's love and the children's caring.

There had to be some way to keep a foot in each world. She'd work on it. She didn't know how, but she would.

For a little while, she had floundered, losing her grasp on her own identity, but now she had found it again. Now she could continue with her life, knowing who she was and what she needed to feel whole again.

She closed her eyes, and cradled in Philip's possessive arms, fell asleep again. Right now she was content.

The next four days passed quickly. The weekend was a wonderful, quiet oasis in the midst of chaos for Jessie. Bright red and green ornaments were unpacked; cranberries and popcorn were strung on thick thread; gingerbread stars were baked and decorated; pine cones were soaked in a salt solution, then left to dry so they could merrily burn in the fireplace later, shooting off colored sparks as they did so.

They shopped for a tree, not too tall but not too small. The children giggled, Jessie laughed, and Philip made wise cracks about coal in stockings and Scrooges and "bah humbugs," all with a definite twinkle in his golden-brown eyes. It was almost a magic time, when things that had pressed upon their lives were set aside so that only *they* were important and only *they* counted. The family was together.

Then came the bright, crisp morning that would lead to Christmas Eve, which the children had been looking forward to so eagerly and Jessie had silently dreaded.

Jessie had given Mrs. Anderson three days off, and all the preparations were up to her. Surprisingly, Philip had joined her and the children to help with the predinner preparations on Christmas Eve. The kitchen rang with the noise of off-key voices singing old carols amid laughter at old jokes and new witticisms.

Even when a fleeting look of sadness crossed Jessie's face as they sang one special carol that P.J. had loved so much, the children and Philip brought her back to the present and the fun they were having. It was no time for maudlin thoughts to mar their family happiness.

By the time Christmas morning came, there was so much going on that Jessie wasn't given a chance to think of the sorrow of not having P.J. with them. The children were ecstatic with their gifts, including the written promise of a trip to Disneyland during the first week of their summer vacation. It had been Philip's gift, but he had carefully checked with Jessie first. Would she come? Jessie's voice had choked as she gave him her answer. She wanted to believe so badly that they would still be together. She had nodded solemnly, and he had kissed her nose, as if words of thanks wouldn't have been enough. They were committed. At least for now.

Once more Philip helped with the initial dinner preparations, then entertained his parents while Jessie helped the children finish the cooking. They were so proud of doing such an important task that Jessie's heart filled with love as she watched them.

Jessie had given Philip a small framed picture of the children for his desk at the office. Philip had loved it, if his reaction was anything to go by.

In return, Philip had given Jessie a small gold heart with both their initials engraved on the back in a style that resembled the block lettering that teenaged boys used to carve their sweethearts' initials on trees. Tears filled her eyes. He had once engraved those same letters on an old tree on campus when they were attending college, and the memories of those days of courtship flooded back to fill her with the joys and the sadness of days gone by.

That night they rested securely in each other's arms as if it were the only place they each dreamed of being. And it was.

Although the spots that covered Amy's little body were still a dull red, her fever was gone, and her spirits had risen. Still, they treated her as if she were still ill. Jessie and Philip had their hands filled keeping her occupied. They played games, told stories and colored in her coloring book.

Beth was also more talkative than she had been in the past. She shyly confided in Jessie about a certain boy in school who always tried to grab and kiss her on the playground. Jessie had to maintain an inquisitive look even though she was dying to chuckle at the boy's antics and ingenious tactics.

Philip finally had to leave Jessie to entertain the children so he could work on a new brief, but more often than not, he found himself following the laughter that had so long been absent in his home, winding up in the den to watch Jessie playing with the children. His eyes glowed with the silent message of his love, but Jessie just wasn't sure whether it was love for his children, the family or her. Where did she fit into his quiet thoughts? Were the reasons he wanted her back good enough to make their marriage a success? Did she really want it to work, or was she, too, chasing rainbows, dreams of what could never be instead of what really was? She didn't know.

Mrs. Anderson had returned late on Sunday, her persimmon face less rigid when she looked in Jessie's direction. Apparently, her opinion of Jessie was slowly—very slowly—changing.

It was the best weekend ever.

Monday morning dawned bright. It was snowing in the sunshine, a southerner's dream of perfect Christmas weather. Beth's transistor radio blared out a Christmas tune that echoed through the house, interrupting everyone's sleep.

Jessie rushed to get through breakfast, almost

wishing she could turn breakfast over to Mrs. Anderson again. Ever since that first morning, the housekeeper had steered clear of the kitchen until Jessie had gone to work. It was better that way, Jessie thought as she virtually threw on her beige wool suit and wine-colored silk blouse, then slipped on her leather pumps. She just wished she had gotten more sleep the night before. A smile crossed her face at the memory. No, forget the sleep. Being in Philip's arms and making love in the middle of the night were too good to pass up even for sleep! She hid a yawn under her hand and ran down the steps. Philip honked just as she reached the door.

"Good-by!" she yelled to no one in particular, and dashed to the car.

Philip smiled at her, an endearing grin that made her warm inside, and she couldn't help but respond.

"I like driving you to work in the morning. It makes an otherwise dreary time far more pleasurable," he said.

"Well, thank you." She kept the mirth from her voice, trying to match her tone to the innocent expression on her face. "It's nice to know I'm a pleasant diversion."

"I didn't mean it that way, and you know it," he growled, but his eyes gleamed in answer to her own. His hand reached over to envelop hers, one finger stroking the palm of her hand into a sensuous awareness.

"Oh?"

"I meant that being alone with you in the early morning is a great way to begin the day." His eyes gleamed with a hidden message that she was quick to interpret, and her heart beat faster with the knowledge. "Not that I can't think of more exciting ways to be alone with you."

She couldn't keep up the innocent act any longer. "I can, too, Philip." Her breath seemed to whoosh from her lungs at the hunger in his eyes. It matched her own.

"We can make it, Jessie. I know we can."

She didn't pretend not to realize what he was talking about. It wasn't the time for games.

"Yes," she said quietly, her blue eyes speaking more eloquently. She loved him, and she thought that he loved her. They could work out their problems—together.

He pulled into the new shopping center and stopped in front of the main entrance. Turning in his seat, he faced her, his hand trailing heat along her shoulder. "I'll pick you up tonight at six."

"I'll be waiting."

Slowly, as if pulled toward her by some invisible rope, he leaned forward and gently touched her parted lips with a soft brushing movement. He could only sip of her sweetness, not drink his fill, if he were going to let them get any work done that day.

"See you then," he promised, his brown eyes searching hers, and all she could do was nod her head in agreement. Her heart was filled with happiness.

Jessie hired three saleswomen, had two more transferred from other stores and successfully saw the clothing transferred to her racks and office supplies unpacked and put in their places. It was a busy day, but one filled with satisfaction. The store opened its doors at ten o'clock, like the rest of the stores, and the crowds began shopping. The day after Christmas was one of the five busiest in the year, and that year was no exception.

Philip was at the curb when she got out at five past six, and he was impatient, if his expression was anything to go by. But when Jessie slid into the seat next to him and placed a quick kiss on his cheek, his impatience disappeared.

"I went home early today." He placed the car in gear and edged it away from the curb and toward the exit.

"Really? I thought you were working on a case that was taking up all your time."

"What do you know about that?" His look was forbidding for just a moment, then turned bland.

"Nothing other than what I just said. That's what you told me this weekend. Why?" She tried to penetrate his calm exterior, knowing there was something he wasn't telling her, but she couldn't tell anything from his expression.

"I just decided to take a small holiday. Besides, I wanted to check on Amy and Beth before I took you out to dinner. I knew you'd worry if I couldn't report with absolute accuracy that they were okay and none the worse for wear when we weren't there."

"Dinner? Lovely," she said, then hesitated before saying, "Thank you for making sure. I know

I'm a little too protective at times. It's just that—"
She couldn't finish.

"P.J.'s death was not your fault, and the girls
won't fade away in our absence." His hand
squeezed hers in reassurance.

"I know. But the memory is always in the back of
my mind."

"And mine. And the girls'."

"I've been pretty selfish, haven't I?" He was
right; she needed to be reminded that she wasn't
the only one who had suffered a loss. They all had.

"No. I think it was just too much for you to
handle at one time. No one can cope with that
much strain and not expect to buckle under it."

"You didn't."

"Yes, I did, but in my own way."

"How?"

"By losing sight of what I loved so much: my
family." His golden eyes turned toward her, captur-
ing and holding her thoughts for a moment before
concentrating once more on the traffic. "In a way,
your moving out was the best thing for both of us. It
gave us time to breathe and realize just what was
important in life. I became closer to my children
than I had ever been before. I saw you in another
light, one that surprised me. By standing away from
you, I saw you in a different role. I realized just how
wonderful you are."

"Thank you, Philip," was all she could manage
to say. It was wonderful for him not to hate her for
deserting him and to put those feelings into words.
This was the perfect time to tell him how much she

loved him, but the words wouldn't come. Some part of her was still too frightened to let them see the light of day.

The restaurant was expecting them. Philip obviously had everything carefully planned, and that thought brought a smile to Jessie's lips as she followed him to their table. That restaurant and that table had been their favorite place to celebrate birthdays and anniversaries over the years.

He had also preordered her favorite entree: Alaskan king crab, with cauliflower and melted cheese on the side. A bottle of chilled white wine sat in a silver ice bucket on a pedestal next to Philip.

A mischievous twinkle lit her eyes. "Are you in a hurry?"

"Yes," was all he answered, but the look she received said it all.

"Is there something going on that I don't know about?"

"Yes," he said again, that same look on his face.

She frowned. "We don't have to go to a party, do we?" Suddenly, she didn't want to share him. She didn't want crowds, or even friends, whom she would have to share him with.

"No party. Just the two of us."

"That's the kind of party I like," she teased, her blue eyes telling him what she had in mind. He smiled in response.

After they left the restaurant, it took Jessie a while to realize that they weren't heading toward home. Philip had positioned her against the length of his body so that her head rested on his shoulder as he drove down Love Boulevard.

She raised her head and stared out the window, noticing her surroundings for the first time. "Where are we going?"

"Someplace where we can be alone."

"But where?" she persisted, suddenly feeling as if she had lost control of the situation.

"Here," he said, as he pulled into a well-lit motel that proclaimed it had waterbeds and cable TV.

A grin flashed across her face as she understood his intention. He couldn't help himself. He kissed her, turning her toward him so he could hold her body as close to his as the seat would allow.

"You're kidnaping me!" she exclaimed in a soft voice.

"Yes," he said huskily, "and I'll keep you until you're willing to give in and accept your fate."

She ran a hand around the back of his neck. "In that case, don't be surprised if I'm never willing."

His golden glance teased her nerves, and his touch sent fire down her spine. "I was hoping you'd say that," he muttered against her neck. "Now stay here and behave yourself like a good captive while I check us in."

Her system hummed with impatience while she awaited his return. She felt like a teenager again! Her hands were clammy, her mouth dry, her heart beating irregularly. Her thoughts drifted back to their dating days, and she could remember having felt that same mixture of anticipation and dread. She had wanted his touch so badly, yet her fear of doing something wrong, of making some stupid move, had seemed to override her pleasure.

She smiled. That wouldn't happen this time.

The room he led her to was cold and slightly damp. The lights on either side of the king-sized waterbed were dim, only allowing Jessie to see the slightly faded pattern of the bedspread. But it was clean, and the bed undulated in small waves, just as it was supposed to.

Philip grinned at her from across the room. He threw the carryall he had hidden in the trunk onto the floor.

"I see you came prepared," Jessie said wryly, glancing at the small suitcase.

"I had to. I didn't want you to wake up in the middle of the night missing your toothbrush and force me to take you home before I changed your mind to match mine."

Jessie walked toward him slowly, only stopping when the tips of her toes touched his. She clasped her arms around his neck. "Oh? And just what am I supposed to change my mind about?"

"About staying with me. Being with me. Always." His voice was gruff and filled with emotion.

"And what makes you think I'd be so hard to persuade?"

"I know you." His eyes filled with remembered pain. "I don't want you to say yes now and change your mind ten minutes later. Once your commitment is made, I'll never let you go, Jessie. I couldn't stand to go through this again."

His arms tightened around her waist, and she could feel the tension in his body as he remained rigid against her. He was controlling his actions, waiting. But for what? The commitment he had spoken of? His next words answered her question.

"I don't want you to say yes or no now. Wait until next week, when Amy is completely better. Give us time, Jessie. We both have changing to do, different ways of seeing things. I just want you to begin thinking about us now, so when the time comes, you'll have a basis for your answer. I don't want any doubts or regrets to creep into our relationship again."

"Agreed," she murmured seductively, touching his lips with hers before sprinkling butterfly kisses all over his jaw and neck. His response was immediate and impossible to hide, and the feeling thrilled her. He couldn't be playing around and still be so aroused by her touch, could he? Stop that! her conscience told her. She was doubting again, and those doubts had tormented her once before. Now was the time for trust.

His hands cupped her buttocks and held her closer to him, knowing she could feel his urgent need. She smiled, pulling at his tie and undoing his shirt buttons. "Are we going to stand here and talk all night, or am I going to be ravished on that waterbed?" Her voice was almost a whisper, but he heard her. His breath escaped in a sigh.

"Oh, ravished, most certainly. What would you like first? I can tie you to the bed with silken scarves, or I can force you into submission with the delicious torment of my teeth and tongue. Which would you prefer?" He pulled out the hem of her blouse and unzipped the back of her skirt, letting it fall to her feet. His hands trembled as he undid the buttons of her blouse.

Jessie wanted to help him, but her hands were

too busy with his shirt. She unsnapped his pants and slowly drew down the zipper. His chest was already bared, and finally, so was the rest of him. They stood facing each other, silently eyeing each other before they spoke.

"I love the way your chest is sprinkled with blond hair," she murmured.

"I love the way your breasts show nothing but creamy skin and a few sun-kissed freckles," he answered.

"I think you have a beautiful set of ribs. And your throat! It's lovely."

"I think yours is lovelier. And your waist. I can span it with my hands now."

"That's because I've lost weight and you have such large, charming hands." She kissed one to show him how charming they were.

"I love the way your hair has so much red in it," he muttered, nuzzling her throat as his hands searched the pleasure points of her slim body.

"And I love your blond hair. It always reminded me of a lion, all tawny and golden."

"I don't know if we're talking at cross-purposes," he began, only to have her give a deep-throated chuckle.

"We aren't," she muttered against his skin. "I know just what you're talking about."

His chuckle answered hers just before he drowned her senses in a deep, loving kiss, his hands tightening to bring her tightly against the fullness of his own taut body.

A moan escaped his lips as he pulled away to

look down at her, searching her face for the same emotions he was feeling.

A small smile, answered by one of Philip's, tugged at Jessie's mouth. "Do you still get seasick?" she asked.

"Not tonight, love," he answered.

The bed undulated as they lay down, the small waves moving them as gently as their hands moved over each other. Philip was on his side, his hand washing over Jessie, finding small indentations and soft spots he had never found before. Why hadn't he noticed that small mole on the side of her hip before? How wonderful she felt beneath him, so complete. How *right!*

His lips followed his wandering hands, teasing, taunting her nipples with small nips before her hands forced his head closer and her lips parted with a moan that told him just how wonderful it felt.

"Do you like this, Jessie?" he murmured, watching her face with intense interest. He moved his hand farther down. "Or do you like this? Tell me, honey. Tell me."

"Yes, that, yes," she answered in response. He was torturing her, and she loved it.

"And what about this? Is this good?"

"Yes."

"Tell me, Jessie. How good?"

"Very good." Her voice was becoming a whisper.

"And this?" His own voice was husky, revealing the depth of his feelings. His lips slowly, tortuously, trailed down her body, stopping to nibble at her waist, her navel, the side of her hip, before resting at the heart of her desire. "Is this good? Tell me, baby. Tell me how you want it so I'll know."

But she couldn't answer with words; her throat was filled with the wonder and joy of their lovemaking, her heart singing with his touch. How could a man, one man, please her beyond the bounds of reality? She didn't know. She didn't care. He was hers, and he loved her. That was all that mattered.

"God, you feel good. So good, so right." His sigh was one of complete and utter pleasure as they merged together. She clasped his lean, hard back to bring him closer to her, into her, hoping she could dissolve and become part of him.

The waterbed undulated late into the night.

9

Jessie kept the memory of their night on the waterbed tucked just inside her head so that at odd moments during the day she could take it out, examine it and love him all over again.

They had gotten home in the early hours of the morning, just in time to eat breakfast and dress for work. Mrs. Anderson had, with a sniff, taken care of cooking for the children. Although the housekeeper hadn't actually said anything in front of Philip, Jessie had tried to smooth things over as best she could, knowing that no matter what she said, Mrs. Anderson would think of her as an unfit mother. She shook her head. So much for charming the world.

She had taken her own car to work that morning because she wanted to return some Christmas presents. Several pieces of clothing hadn't fit the girls and needed to be exchanged. By the time she reached home, she was exhausted. The traffic had been bad, but she had managed to miss half of it!

"Philip," she called from the front door. But instead of Philip, Mrs. Anderson came out of the kitchen, wiping her hands on her apron.

"Mr. Young isn't home yet. He called to say he'd be an hour or so late."

"Thank you, Mrs. Anderson." Jessie continued to smile even though she was disappointed. Her thoughts had been with Philip all day long.

The phone rang, and she reached for it before Mrs. Anderson could get her hands untangled from her apron.

"Young residence," she said, copying the older woman's words and manner of speaking.

"Is Philip home yet, or is he still at the office?" a melodious voice questioned imperiously, and Jessie's heart thumped down to her feet. Her blood stopped circulating. Her mind went blank. "Hello? Are you there, Mrs. Anderson? Answer me!"

"Yes, I'm here, Miss Sinclair," Jessie said in a monotone.

"Who is this? Jessie?"

"Yes," Jessie answered shortly, not about to give the woman any more information than she had to.

A soft chuckle reverberated through the phone and sent a cold lightning bolt through Jessie's system. "Well, well, the little wife has decided to come home, after all. Is Philip pleased or just tolerating your presence? Or do you even know?"

Jessie's voice was tight with anger. "Is there something you wanted me to tell him, Catherine?"

"Just tell him that I'll meet him in my suite around nine-thirty tomorrow morning. He'll know what I'm talking about." Her soft, kittenish voice was filled with a light, airy quality that spelled trouble for Jessie's nerves.

"I'll be sure to tell him. Good-by." It took every ounce of strength Jessie had not to slam the phone down in the singer's ear, but she managed—barely.

Her entire body vibrated with the hate she felt toward the woman. Was he still representing her, or was he representing someone else and just playing around with her? She remembered the previous night. No, he couldn't be playing around! His love was too real, too intense, for him to have another woman on the side. But no matter how hard she tried to prevent them, all the nagging doubts that had once been so much a part of her life flowed back with a vengeance, making her feel short, fat and dumpy once more.

She walked toward the kitchen, intent on asking Mrs. Anderson how often Catherine Sinclair called until she realized just how much the housekeeper might enjoy giving her the answer. Jessie suddenly stopped. Why should she give the other woman the satisfaction of seeing her upset? She would calmly, rationally, confront Philip and ask him to explain. After all, he had asked her to trust him. Since she had moved back into the house, he had answered every question she had asked. So she should trust in his answers now. That was it. She needed to be calm and wait for what she was sure would be a logical explanation.

Unclenching her hands with an effort, she turned and walked back to the living room. A good stiff drink would be in order while she waited for Philip to come home. It would also give her something to do while she tried to bring her anger under control again. She hoped. She poured herself a stiff scotch, added two ice cubes and decided against water. If it was good enough for Philip, it was good enough for her.

By the time Philip walked in, half an hour later, Jessie had had two potent drinks. Her logic had weakened beyond belief, but her anger hadn't fled; it had grown. How dare he make love to her, then go to that woman! How dare he not tell her about representing that . . . that . . . singer! How dare he, period!

She stood on wobbly high heels and confronted him before he even had a chance to kiss her. "How dare you come to me straight from that tramp Catherine Sinclair!"

His face showed surprise, as he measured her anger. "Probably because I didn't just come from her. I came from the office." His voice was calm and composed, but the swallow he took after he spoke was all the evidence Jessie needed.

"I don't mean just now. I mean sometime in the past! Besides, the hell you didn't! I just saw you gulp! You only gulp when you're lying!" she accused.

"All right, Jessie. Tell me what happened and I'll give you an explanation."

"Your girl friend called and wants you to meet her in her hotel suite at nine-thirty tomorrow morning; that's what happened!"

"And you automatically assumed I was taking her to bed."

Her chin came up determinedly. Although her blue eyes glistened with unshed tears, her body was rigid with stubborn anger. "Are you going to talk me out of it? Tell me I'm imagining things? That Catherine Sinclair doesn't want your body? That you don't want her for a sexy little playmate?"

Philip ran a hand through his golden hair. Exasperation was plain on his face. "No. I'm not going to tell you anything. This time I'm going to let *you* figure it out and come up with the answers. You seem to do that, anyway."

He took a seat in the thickly upholstered chair across from her and leaned his head back, closing his eyes. He looked so tired. Exhausted. Memories of the previous night burned through her mind. No wonder! They'd been up half the night! She frowned. They'd both been making mad, passionate love into the early morning.

She tried to focus on his face, but it was too hard. She focused on his tie instead. "Philip?" Her voice was low, hesitant, begging for words of comfort and understanding. Her ankle twisted, and she plopped down on the couch again. "Philip?"

He sighed, keeping his eyes closed. "What, Jessie?"

"Did you have her for your playmate?"

"No, Jessie."

"Oh."

He opened one eye. "Is that it? Oh? Aren't you going to tell me I'm lying? Aren't you going to scream at me for being unfaithful?"

Memories of all the nights they had shared during the past week filtered through her dazed mind. He had been home on time every evening that week, and every night they had made love. He had called her at least once a day, telling her how wonderful she was, how adorable she looked, how sexy she felt. Nothing he had done had given her the slightest reason to doubt that he loved her. Her mind buzzed, her sight blurred, and she held a shaking hand to her forehead to still the pounding there.

"Is she your client?"

"Yes."

"Why, Philip?" Her voice shook, but she couldn't stop herself from asking.

"She's a witness to a drug charge against a very prominent politician. I began the case last summer. If I'm lucky, this week should be the end of it."

She sat quietly, suddenly remembering Philip and Noah Weston talking about a party that Catherine Sinclair had attended almost two years earlier. One of the men had been caught with drugs, and Noah had asked Philip's help in keeping it quiet but proceeding with the case. Philip had agreed. She remembered it now. With the wheels of justice moving as slowly as they sometimes did, it all made sense.

Her next question shocked him into opening both eyes.

"Philip?" she asked in a soft voice. "Am I pretty?"

"Beautiful."

"Sexy?"

"More than any other woman I know."

"Silly?"

"Very. But for some reason I can't explain, I love you, anyway."

She tried a small, wobbly smile. "Really?"

He leaned forward, taking both her hands in his. "Really. But don't take my word for it. Ask the people I work with, my mother, my father, Mrs. Anderson, the children. I have all sorts of character references who'll tell you that I've always loved you." His fingers gently soothed the palms of her hands, relaxing her with their warm pressure.

She blinked hard. "And I'm being foolish, right?"

"Wrong."

She blinked again. "Wrong?" Her voice sounded like the small squeak of a frightened mouse. She cleared her throat and tried again. "Wrong?" She looked at him, only to see a wealth of golden warmth in his eyes as he watched her changing expressions.

"I don't want you to retreat from me again or cut me out of your mind. That's what you did the last time. I couldn't stand that. As long as you're jealous, I know you care."

"You want me to be jealous of everyone in your life?" She sniffed, and he chuckled, pulling out a pristine handkerchief to help her wipe her nose.

"Yes. I love it when you're jealous. It tells me you care."

"But I've always been jealous of you! You're too gorgeous for your own good. I often wondered why you ever married me. Compared to you, I look like a 'before' in a glamour-clinic ad."

He leaned over and gently kissed her lips. "Stop fishing for compliments. You look terrific, and you know it."

"No, I don't. I need you to tell me so."

His brows rose. "It's nice to know I'm needed for something. I never thought you needed anyone. You were always so self-sufficient."

"I was never that. I only pretended to be because you always were. I wanted to be you, live through you."

His golden eyes bored into hers. "And now, Jessie? Do you still want to be me?"

Her smile was tinged with the glimmer of a new self-awareness. "No." She hesitated as her thoughts formed some semblance of order, then went on. "Now I want to be me, only better."

"How so?"

"Well, I want to be your only shining star, but I also want to be mine." Suddenly, she realized what she had said, and her eyes opened wide. "Is that how you feel about me, Philip? That you want to be the center of my universe, yet you also want to live your own life and be your own person?"

He nodded, understanding her. "Yes. I wanted you to revolve around me, but I couldn't take the time to reciprocate. I needed my work to be a success in my own mind as well as for the money."

His lips twitched with a rueful grin. "But I never expected to be in what I thought was your position in our marriage."

She stared just over his left shoulder, her blue eyes growing even wider. Her mouth formed an "oh," and Philip could almost see the proverbial light bulb over her head.

"How odd," she said in a whisper. "And now you're in my old position, and I'm sitting in yours." Her eyes came back to him. "Well, not quite. I'm only a lowly manager, but someday—"

"Oh, Jessie." He gave a mock groan. "I think you like the idea of me suffering while you decide what you're going to do with the rest of our lives."

A dimple appeared, indenting her cheeks and giving her an impish quality. Her eyes twinkled mischievously. "You're right. I like watching you squirm."

"In that case, come upstairs to our room and I'll show you how good I am at it," he teased, giving her hands a light squeeze. His eyes were sending a more intimate message, one that made her heart skip a beat.

"Not on your life! The children are in the kitchen helping Mrs. Anderson make cookies and would be shocked at their father's behavior. Besides, you haven't eaten yet, and I waited to eat with you. Now I'm starved."

"I offer you Mount Olympus, and you give me mangoes and papayas." He stood, pulling her out of her seat and into his arms. Placing a kiss on her nose, he asked, "Are you still angry with me?"

"No," she said softly, pushing aside the doubts

167

that had lingered so long. She would face them later and tear them apart one by one. But not now. Right now she wanted to enjoy his company, his touch, his presence. The next day would come soon enough.

They walked arm in arm past the gaily lit Christmas tree and made their way toward the giggling voices in the kitchen. The rest of their family was waiting for them.

Philip sat naked in the shaft of moonlight that came through their bedroom window. He had pulled the small bedroom chair up to the foot of the bed, and his feet were carefully propped on the end of the mattress as he watched Jessie sleep. It was three in the morning, and he was exhausted, but he couldn't sleep. Watching Jessie was the next best thing to holding her in his arms.

He loved her. God! How he loved her! Why had he realized how deep his love for her was only after he had nearly lost her?

She turned in her sleep and gave a soft sigh. A small smile barely touched her lips. Was it for him? Was she remembering, however briefly, their love-making? He hoped so. He wanted to fill her so completely with himself that there would be no room for anyone else in her life. His heart gave a heavy thump in his chest as he thought of Jay Peckman's look the night of the Toodies' party. The man wanted her! It had been written all over his face! Philip had had to restrain himself from punching the guy out just on general principles.

He unclenched his hands. Well, he would have

the last laugh. Jessie was his. All he had to do was convince her of that fact. Once she was thoroughly committed to him and their marriage, she would never leave him again.

A glimmer of a smile touched his mouth. Over the past months, she had changed in so many ways. Who would have thought that not only could she manage a clothing store but also the salesladies? He had certainly underestimated her all along. But that would change. Now he knew just how limited a mold he had placed her in, and although their children meant the world to both of them, Jessie shouldn't be penalized for needing other, adult stimulation. As long as that stimulation excluded all other men except Philip! He had rarely been jealous since he had married her, but he was now! Fool! But unlike Jessie, who used to run at the first sign of any kind of confrontation, he wasn't afraid to fight for what he wanted. In fact, he relished it. Just let anyone come between him and Jessie and he'd kill for her!

Shifting his feet, Philip leaned forward, watching the shadows play across her face. She was so very beautiful, and she didn't know it. Oh, not beautiful in the classic sense, like Catherine Sinclair or his secretary Lainie, but in another, more subtle yet powerful way. His heart swelled, and his veins warmed with the intense emotions that were aroused when he thought of her as his. He was so damn proud!

The fleeting thought of his secretary and Catherine Sinclair brought a frown to his forehead. The following day was the last session in closed court with Catherine; then the jury would deliberate and hand down a verdict. His secretary would be attending to make sure that everything was buttoned up tight, so he could walk away from the case with a clear conscience and never look back. He wanted nothing more to do with the singer. She was a prime bitch, and he had almost played her fool. Thank goodness his own instincts had kept him away from her!

And his secretary—now there was another problem that had to be attended to promptly. Until he and Jessie had separated, he hadn't realized that Jessie had been jealous of the woman. But in opening his mind to that possibility, he had also opened his eyes. Jessie was right. All the signals Lainie had thrown out lately would have awakened the dead, and the only reason Philip had missed them was because he was so caught up in trying to resurrect his marriage. After the trial was over, he'd take both Catherine and Lainie to lunch, which was customary. Then, in the afternoon, he would release Lainie. She'd have no problem finding employment; she was an excellent legal secretary. But he didn't want anything to interfere with his marriage to Jessie. Not anything.

He climbed back into bed, and Jessie unconsciously snuggled close to him, sharing her warmth. His lips caressed the riot of red curls, his arms tightening possessively.

After the next day, his business life would be in order, and his personal life would be on the road to recovery. He hoped.

* * *

Jay Peckman lounged against the counter of Jessie's almost completely stocked store. "Since you're so far ahead of schedule, why don't you take a busman's holiday and go finish your after-Christmas exchanging? Everything seems under control here."

Jessie looked at him suspiciously, teasing him with her serious expression. "Why? Are you going to dock my paycheck?"

"Because you aren't needed right now, but you'll have your feet worked off next week when the first clothing shipments arrive here direct from the factory instead of going to the other stores to be readied. And no, I won't dock your paycheck." He spread his hands in the air, a rueful smile on his face. "Can't I do something nice once in a while without everyone looking for an ulterior motive?"

She chuckled. "Of course you can. I just wondered, that's all."

"Well, if you really don't want the day off, why don't you have lunch with me? I'm wonderful, a smart dresser and have a lavish expense account."

Reaching under the counter for her purse, she laughed again. "No, thanks. I know just what I'm going to do." She turned quickly and headed toward the back office and the phone. "Philip ought to be breaking for lunch in another half hour or so. I'll surprise him."

"Me and my damn fool mouth," Jay muttered to himself, hungrily watching the sway of her hips as she moved through the store.

"Is Mr. Young in?" Jessie asked quickly when she

got through to Philip's office and registered the fact that Lainie wasn't on the other end. Where was she? Not too far from Philip, Jessie bet.

"I'm sorry, but Mr. Young isn't here right now. May I take a message?" Apparently, one of the younger assistants was manning the phones.

"Yes, tell him his wife called and wants to meet him for lunch. I'll be at work."

"He already has a reservation at the Chez Marie at one o'clock today, Mrs. Young."

"Oh?" Suddenly, an alarm went off in her head. "Who's dining with him?"

"Lainie's the only one I know of, ma'am," the young voice answered obediently.

"I see," Jessie said slowly. "Forget the message, then. Thank you." She released the phone with difficulty. Her breath had stopped, caught somewhere between her empty lungs and her aching heart.

She moved like a sleepwalker as she headed toward her car, ignoring the odd looks of her coworkers and the knowing look of her boss. She had taken the car again that morning, having explained to Philip that she might be late getting home again.

And now he would be with Lainie all day. In a little over an hour, they would be cozily ensconced in a dark corner of an exclusive restaurant, sharing murmured words of . . . of what? Endearment or business? Her mind told her it was business, but her rioting emotions said otherwise. Despite her best intentions, she still didn't trust him, and not knowing scared the wits out of her.

One thought crunched down on another, and another, hitting her bruised brain like rocks in an avalanche. Had he been making love to that woman in the early-morning light of some shabby motel? No, that wasn't his style. A classy, secluded hotel with room service was more like Philip, and definitely more like Lainie, who was not only intelligent and witty but beautiful as well. Much prettier than Jessie could ever be. Ever.

Without realizing it, Jessie had driven to the cemetery where P.J. was buried. The air was damp and cold, but she didn't feel it as she stepped onto the winding, rocky path. The ground was cold and wet, as if it had rained earlier and the moisture had remained suspended in the air and on the grass. She sat down next to P.J.'s gravestone and leaned her head against the lifeless marble.

She was too numb to cry.

She had to face facts, both about herself and her marriage.

All their married life she had been unconsciously waiting for another woman to come and steal her husband away. She had never seen herself as Philip obviously had. He had always said that she was beautiful, charming, wonderful. But she had believed that someday someone else would come along and pull the wool from his eyes, allowing him to see her for what she was: frumpy, not witty, but sharp tongued and cute. Cute! How she hated that word! Inside her five foot two, slightly plump body was a five foot eight woman, slender as a gazelle and as beautiful as the Mona Lisa, and all people could say about her was that she was *cute!*

She shifted. The next day would be New Year's Eve, a time for celebrating the coming of the new year and reminiscing about the old one. A tidal wave of self-pity washed over her, and she shuddered with the impact. The past year and a half had been for her the worst year ever. And if she left Philip forever, all she had to look forward to was an apartment that housed her few belongings and an aching loneliness as big as all outdoors.

She finally stood, her muscles stiff with cold, and stared down at P.J.'s marker. After her son had died, her life had twisted into something she couldn't recognize anymore. Looking back, Jessie realized that she had felt the guilt of his death all along. She had accused herself of being lazy by being part of a car pool, of not driving that day. She had even silently accused Philip of paying so much attention to work that he wasn't home to take his son to the baseball game, as some of the other fathers did. But the truth of the matter was that there was no sense in wondering what might have been, and to lay blame on anyone was past being silly; it was selfish.

Since then, she had indulged in one selfish action after another, running away from what she didn't want to confront and then blaming her running on others. She had never fought for what she wanted: It either fell in her lap, or she didn't get it.

Her head snapped up. She had never even fought for Philip. Even when they were dating. Never.

But she would now. Philip was hers! If they were ever going to make their marriage work, it would take the two of them fighting together against the world and its sins, not just Philip attempting to protect her in some small, peaceful kingdom.

She stared down at her son's grave. "I love you, P.J., and I always will. No one will ever take your place in my heart, but I have others to love and care for, too. I almost forgot that in my grief," she murmured, tears catching in her throat. "I'll be back later." Her promise froze in the cold wind as she turned and ran back toward the car.

If she hurried, she could reach home, change and crash Philip's intimate little luncheon. This time, she refused to remain weak and meek. All her life she had accepted whatever fell into her lap, good or bad. But now was a time for change. She couldn't accept what the fates had in store for her. She wanted Philip more than she had ever wanted anything, and this time she was going to fight for what she wanted. No more watching others walk away with the prize! No more running when things got rough! She was different now—a woman who wasn't going to lose gracefully again!

10

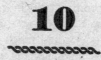

Makeup, delicately applied, and a blue dress that the saleslady had assured her was "dynamite" were Jessie's armor as her trembling legs took her to Chez Marie's door.

Second, third and fourth thoughts assailed her, but her legs refused to move in any direction but forward.

Please don't rebuff me, Philip, was her silent prayer as she pushed the door open and walked in, attempting to look as if she were five foot eight and svelte. It wasn't working. It took more imagination than she had to pretend she was something she wasn't.

Before the maître d' had time to approach her, Jessie spotted Philip sitting at an intimate table for four—and he was seated with both Lainie and

Catherine Sinclair. Jessie had cajoled herself into believing she could handle one. But two?

"Feet, don't fail me now," she muttered, plastering a smile that more closely resembled a grimace on her face. She headed for his table, hoping she would make it across the room without turning and running away in the opposite direction. How could she have talked herself into such a crazy scheme?

But it was too late to back out now. Philip's slightly bored expression evaporated right before her eyes. His blond head snapped up, and his golden-brown eyes grew wide and wary. Her smile broadened as her sense of bravado grew. Surely Philip wouldn't let those women tear her limb from limb. It wouldn't look good in front of the other diners.

She straightened her shoulders, marching toward him with grim determination. Someone had once told her that in a time of crisis she should ask herself what was the worst thing that could happen. Losing Philip was the answer. But she'd lose him, anyway, if she walked out of the restaurant and out of his life, so she really had nothing to lose.

He stood, holding his napkin in his hand, as she reached his side and gazed up in adoration, tilting her head slightly so their audience of two could see her loving expression. "Hello, darling," she murmured in an intimately husky voice. "I couldn't let you immerse yourself in business today without my seeing you." She hesitated for effect, not willing to admit, even to herself, that her voice had faltered for a split second. "Not after last night."

His guarded but resigned expression told her that he had absolutely no idea what fireworks would erupt next, but he was going to brave his way through the ordeal until the bitter end. "Wonderful, sweetheart. Come and sit next to me and we'll have the waiter bring another menu," he said with more aplomb than she would have given him credit for. So both of them were capable of dealing out surprises!

"Thank you, darling," she murmured sweetly, accepting the seat he pulled out. She smiled benignly at the other women, whose eyes shot poisoned darts in her direction. Her heart plummeted to the bottoms of her new sling-back shoes. They had probably been at each other's throats until she had come on the scene. Now they would unite against her! She stiffened her spine. Well, just let them! She was ready—she hoped.

She hid her shaking hands beneath the table. "And how has life been treating you, Catherine? Has Philip resolved that mess you got yourself into?"

Catherine smiled like a well-fed tigress. "Philip handled it beautifully, as he does every other problem in my life." She rested her hand on his arm, giving it a squeeze before she daintily withdrew her touch.

Jessie gave a quick coy glance at Philip, her lashes hiding the barb she would have loved to deliver. Instead, she turned a wide-eyed look to Catherine. "And I'm sure you must have a multitude of problems. Some people just can't seem to cope very well." Her eyes widened even more. "I didn't realize *you* fell into that category, though. I'm sorry."

"Don't feel sorry for me, Jessie. Find others to feel sorry for. Those who have no reason to exist from day to day." Catherine's eyes gleamed with malice. "Those whose only use might be in doing someone else's dirty work or being a welcome mat for everyone else to wipe their feet on."

Out of the corner of her eye, Jessie saw Philip lean forward to put a stop to Catherine's barbs, and her heart sang. He was going to defend her! Suddenly, contrarily, she didn't want to be defended. She *wanted* to play this dangerous game.

Jessie laid a restraining hand on Philip's sleeve, then leaned forward. "Oh, Catherine, how right you are! Perhaps now that you've learned that particular lesson yourself, you'll be better able to cope with life." Jessie gave a mock sigh. "So many people, especially women, don't seem to understand that to be needed and to be wanted are two different things. An attorney needs his clients, but a husband wants his wife. If he didn't, he would get divorced."

"I wasn't speaking of myself," Catherine said stiffly.

Jessie's eyes widened, then darted to Lainie. "You can't mean Lainie?" she said, acting as if she were shocked to the core. "Why, Lainie is the most levelheaded and determined woman I know! I'm sure Lainie knows the difference between need and want. Why, she works so hard for Philip and hardly gets anything for it except a pay check every two weeks! Half the time Philip doesn't even give her credit for all the dreary, mundane day-to-day work she does. He just takes it for granted that she'll be good at her job and not make waves in the office."

Both women gasped.

Jessie finally cast a look in Philip's direction, frightened of his response to her irresponsible behavior. Instead, she saw him lean back, a bright grin on his face that could have rivaled the sun. His golden eyes twinkled with mirth as he barely managed to check an explosion of laughter. He was enjoying every moment of this! Three women fighting over him as if they were alley cats and he was the only trash can in town!

Suddenly, Jessie met and held Philip's eyes. He touched her knee under the table and gave it a light caress before forcing his attention back to the two obviously shocked women. They had known Jessie for years, and this woman was a stranger! It was as if they had expected Betty Crocker and gotten the Wicked Witch of the West!

Philip nodded to each of them. "Lainie, you have the company credit card, don't you?" When she nodded slowly, he continued. "Here are my car keys. Drop Catherine off wherever she wants and leave my car at the office. Oh, and please feel free to have whatever you want for lunch. I have to take my wife home and punish her properly for her behavior today. If you'll excuse us . . . ." He rose and practically lifted Jessie from her seat.

But Catherine wasn't finished yet. She had finally retrieved some of her composure. "Really, Philip, I thought men didn't beat their wives anymore," she chided in a deep, loaded-with-sex voice.

"The punishment I have in mind requires only the furnishings of our master bedroom." His tone was low; his loving look toward his wife said it all.

Jessie was stunned. They walked around the tables to the large reception area, sedately decorated with mistletoe and holly and an all-gold tree in the corner. Philip had never openly held so intimate a conversation with her before! Never! In a crowd he would usually be as big a stuffed shirt as the rest of them!

The maître d' stopped them just as they reached the door. "Mr. Young? Was everything all right? Have we displeased you?" he asked worriedly.

Philip turned, then looked down at Jessie, who stood by his side. Her legs were shaking with reaction. "Everything was fine, André, just fine. It's just that I prefer the company of my wife. *Alone.*"

Philip broke into rich, unsuppressed laughter, a deep, vibrant sound that Jessie felt tingling all the way down to her toes. His eyes were warm with mirth as he watched her stunned reaction. Damn! It felt good to see her become totally surprised by his actions! He knew she felt that too many times he was too rigid, too stuffy, and now he knew what she had meant when she had said loosen up. Surprising Jessie also had its advantages. For once, she didn't have a quick comeback or smart remark. That called for one more surprise tactic.

Without giving her time to recover, Philip swung her into his arms, and his lips came down on hers. His arms tightened as he held her molded into him, and his mouth did crazy things to her. The kiss was over practically before it had begun, leaving Jessie with an unreal feeling that what had transpired was all part of a nightmare that had turned into a lover's dream. She smiled. So what? She certainly wasn't going to pinch herself and wake up.

"I love you, Jessie Young. I love you so much I'd go through that whole debacle again just to please your new-found sense of confidence."

Philip's arm came around to cradle her next to him as he pushed open the door and led her outside, hustling her toward her car.

Philip drove with the assurance that years of battling traffic had given him. Jessie sat upright, suddenly shy as she realized just how much of a witch she had been. A smile crossed her lips as she remembered the hate and jealousy she had seen in both women's eyes.

She had won! She had fought the most formidable enemy a woman can fight, the other woman, and had come out of the battle not only the victor but unscarred.

"I was so proud of you. I never dreamed that you would fight for me. You always ran from disagreeable situations before, but this time you were relentless!" He glanced at her and she grinned at the knowledge that he was right.

She saw, she fought, she conquered. But the mere fact of her conquering wasn't as important as the fact that she had stayed to fight instead of running, as she usually did.

"Quit grinning. You won, but winners should never gloat," Philip said, breaking into her thoughts.

"I did win, didn't I?" She giggled impudently, suddenly relaxed and finally feeling as tall and slender as she had dreamed. She was a veritable Greek goddess. "To the victor go the spoils." She crooked her arm through his, resting her head against his neatly tailored dark suit.

"Are you saying I'm spoiled?" His mock angry tone made her giggle instead of tremble. Suddenly, she felt as light as a balloon.

"No, darling." She soothed the crease in his pant leg with a long nail, delighting in the tensing of his muscles. "But you used to be."

"So were you."

"Don't you like me better this way?"

"I love you any way I can get you."

"But . . ." Her forehead creased as she frowned. Suddenly, she was unsure again.

"No buts. If you think working is the answer for you, then I'll have to adjust. If you need Mrs. Anderson—"

"We, darling. If we need Mrs. Anderson," she interrupted, not wanting him to assign her full responsibility for their need to take on help with the children.

"We," he corrected. "If we need Mrs. Anderson to continue with us, then we'll have her. And if you can fight the rest of our lives like you just did in Chez Marie, then I won't have to worry about predatory females. I'll just tell them about my jealous warrior wife."

She arched a disbelieving brow in his direction. It was all he needed to pull the car to a halt in a small side street. Turning toward her, he kissed her.

"Do you really think that would stop a predatory, man-seeking woman from making her self-appointed rounds? You're confusing her with the mailman! A woman is much more single-minded than that." She glanced around. They were nowhere near home. In fact, they were less than a block from her apartment. "Where are we going?"

"To your place." By the time he answered, the car was once more in motion. In no time, he was slipping into a vacant spot in the parking lot. "I have a great need to be alone with you, and this is the only place we can go where no one can interfere."

The small rooms felt lonely. The apartment had been exactly what she had needed, somewhere where she could lick her wounds so she could continue to grow and eventually come to understand herself and those she loved. It had served its purpose.

Hours later, the small apartment was filled with the scent of freshly brewed coffee. Low, sensuous music played in the background. Jessie and Philip stood naked by the window, his arms circling her waist to lie on her slim abdomen, his chin resting on the top of her head.

"Happy New Year, Mrs. Young." He lowered his head and nuzzled a sensitive spot on her neck.

"It isn't the new year yet," she answered breathlessly. His hands had begun to move along a trail that was as familiar as it was exciting.

"It's after midnight. That makes it New Year's Eve."

"Oh." She reached up to hold his shoulders and

turned in his arms. "Then by all means wish me Happy New Year, although I have a feeling that I won't ever have to worry about being happy again."

His voice was low in her ear. "I'm so glad we didn't make plans for tonight. Now I can celebrate our new marriage and the new year—alone."

Jessie sighed, giving herself up to the feelings that sang through her blood. He touched her body, her mind, her senses. Her instincts, though long buried, had been right. They belonged together.

"I love you," she murmured, snuggling more tightly into the curve of his torso. "I know we're going to be happy for the rest of our lives."

He grinned, but his expression had a tinge of sadness, too. "I wish I could promise you all the happiness in the world. But even if I could, after today, I'd say that you'd turn it down. You'd want to do it, find it, create it, by yourself."

"And then I'd want to share it with you." Her hands cupped his jaw. "Is that so terrible? Isn't that what you want to do, too?"

"Yes, love."

Jessie sighed. "Funny," she said, glancing up as her hands began their own journey along his lean body. "Before, I felt as if I had lost something that I couldn't recapture. But I don't feel that way now. I know what it was I lost. I lost your love."

"You never lost it, darling. It was just misplaced for a while. But you have it now, and you'll have it for always."

"I love you, Philip." She could finally say it without doubts.

"And I love you." He held her close, kissing the top of her head before smiling broadly. "You're one terrific lady, Mrs. Young."

She sighed contentedly. "Thank goodness you said it. I thought I was going to have to write a list of pluses, telling you just how great I am and all that I have to offer the right man."

He chuckled. "The only man, Jessie."

"The only man," she echoed before tilting her head for his kiss.

That kiss proved without a doubt the depth of his love, and Jessie spoke without words her answering endearment.

Silhouette Desire
15-Day Trial Offer

A new romance series that explores contemporary relationships in exciting detail

Six Silhouette Desire romances, free for 15 days! We'll send you six new Silhouette Desire romances to look over for 15 days, absolutely free! If you decide not to keep the books, return them and owe nothing.

Six books a month, free home delivery. If you like Silhouette Desire romances as much as we think you will, keep them and return your payment with the invoice. Then we will send you six new books every month just as soon as they are published — even before they are in the bookstores. You get the convenience of Home Delivery and we pay the postage and handling each month. There are no minimum number of books to buy and you can cancel at any time.

Mail this coupon today.

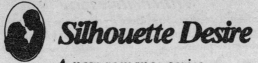

Silhouette Desire

*A new romance series
that explores
contemporary relationships
in exciting detail*

*Here are two of your favorite authors
and their complete list
of Desire titles!*

Stephanie James

_____	CORPORATE AFFAIR	No. 1/$1.95
_____	VELVET TOUCH	No. 11/$1.95
_____	LOVE IN PURSUIT	No. 19/$1.95
_____	RENAISSANCE MAN	No. 25/$1.95
_____	RECKLESS PASSION	No. 31/$1.95
_____	PRICE OF SURRENDER	No. 37/$1.95
_____	AFFAIR OF HONOR	No. 49/$1.95
_____	TO TAME THE HUNTER	No. 55/$2.25
_____	GAMEMASTER	No. 67/$2.25

Suzanne Simms

_____	OF PASSION BORN	No. 17/$1.95
_____	A WILD SWEET MAGIC	No. 43/$1.95
_____	ALL THE NIGHT LONG	No. 61/$2.25

Silhouette Desire
320 Steelcase Rd. E., Markham,
Ontario L3R 2M1

Please send me the books I have checked above. I am enclosing a total of $_____ (Please add 75 cents for postage & handling.) My cheque or money order is enclosed. (No cash or C.O.D.'s please.)

Name_____

Address_____Apt._____

City_____

Prov._____ Postal Code_____

Prices subject to change without notice.   (DBD2)